A CLOWN'S EULOGY

A CLOWN'S EULOGY

KIRK TINSLEY

© 2018 Kirk Tinsley

All rights reserved. No portion of this book may be reproduced, stored in a retrieval system, or transmitted in any form or by any means—electronic, mechanical, photocopy, recording, scanning, or other—without the prior written permission of the copyright holder.

Author's note: This novel is a work of fiction. Names, characters, places, and incidents are either products of the author's imagination or used fictitiously. Any sim-ilarity to people living or dead is purely coincidental.

Scripture quotations are taken from the Holy Bible, New International Version®, NIV® Copyright ©1973, 1978, 1984, 2011 by Biblica, Inc.® Used by permission. All rights reserved worldwide.

This book is dedicated to my amazing wife,
Lina, and our three boys,
Kael, Elyas, and Levi,
for their unwavering support and love

We run away from situations thinking we can escape the unpleasantness—only to discover that the unpleasantness is us.

—*Julie Ackerman*

ONE

Nothing makes us as lonely as our secrets.
—*Paul Tournier*

Gaston Jones was a fraud.

Even before the plane's rapid descent, he had reached that conclusion by page 58 of *The Myths of Big Tent Entertainment: Inside the Ringling Brothers, Barnum & Bailey Circus*. On a whim, he had picked up the book from a newsstand—Hudson News, to be exact—at the Atlanta International Airport while waiting for his connecting flight to Charlotte on the third-day leg of a four-day business trip. So far, he'd hit three major cities—Memphis, Orlando, and Atlanta—where he'd met with some of his primary policyholders. He was set to finish up in Raleigh, home of his biggest client, before finally heading back home to Hernando. But even that much time away would not be long enough to deal with the discovery he had just made. He was a gen-u-ine, certified fake. And no matter what anyone else thought—including Conner, his biggest fan—it was true. Man! Whoever would have thought it would come to this?

As far back as Gaston could remember, he had been fascinated by clowns and the way they made people feel. The perpetual smiles on their painted faces. The oversized shoes. The huge red noses. The outlandish outfits. Was there something behind all this? He had always loved watching the jokesters make the audience laugh at the Memphis Civic Center when the circus came to town—juggling, dancing awkwardly, dashing out of the ring to run into the crowd, then disappearing, leaving them wanting more. Yeah, pretty cool. Don't all kids dream of running away to join the circus?

One thing he knew, though: His life *was* a circus, and his smile was as painted on as any clown's he'd ever seen. He had long faked a pretentious, happy lifestyle while hiding out behind a proverbial mask. Just like a clown, he existed to perform, to make people happy, to lift their spirits, if only temporarily. But at forty-seven, he hadn't exactly become a clown . . . unless the term could be applied to the infrequent, lame jokes he cracked at the bimonthly chamber meetings. Or to his occasional "clowning" around at Big Ernie's Bar. More and more a pattern had revealed itself. Charming to friends and strangers, Gaston had developed a skilled routine of defer and deflect—quickly returning to that well-known place of making people believe and admire.

Gaston had perfected his role. He knew how to dress to impress, but he didn't feel impressive. Even though acting president Jim Edmunds had just named him the Kiwanis Charter Member of the Year, he could hardly accept the award with gratitude, as his attention quickly turned to his battle within. Surrounded by a huge crowd and loud applause, Gaston had teared up during the awards ceremony—but not for the reason most people in the audience assumed. *Are they here to see the real me?* he had wondered. *Or the person they believe me to be?*

From his first-class window seat, Gaston stared off into space . . . a space where the view always seemed to be clouded with boredom and misery. The corporate world had never appealed to him the way he had hoped, but it was his bread and butter, at least for now. Entertaining clients came naturally and brought its own reward—some superficial laughs and a kind of anonymity that kept him at a comfortable, safe distance. But at the end of the day, what could he take home to his lonely bachelor pad—his ten private, picturesque acres down Mill Hollow Road? Hernando, Mississippi—his birthplace and the town where most of his family lived—had been named one of *Money* magazine's "100 Best Places to Live" . . . yet even his hometown, and everything else he called his own, had lost its savor. How could a life that was supposed to be so good become such a circus?

Amid a whirlwind of a trip, he was beginning to feel a little jet-lagged, to say the least. The darkness outside his window made visible the lights of the cities and towns below, illuminated by the bright, blinking beacons on the plane's wing. As he looked downward, his musings were interrupted by the friendly voice of a flight attendant. "Ladies and gentlemen, we have started our descent. In preparation for landing, please make sure your seat backs and tray tables are in their full upright position, your seatbelt is securely fastened, and all carry-on luggage is stowed beneath the seat in front of you or in the overhead bins . . ." As he'd done a thousand times, he stashed his book in the seat pocket and readied himself for the long grind ahead before the wheels of the MD-80 touched down on the tarmac.

When the big plane rolled to a complete stop after taxiing to Gate 31, Gaston glanced at his watch—11:25 p.m. EST. By the time he collected his luggage, picked up his rental car, and got a bite to eat, it would be a very late night. And there was a two-and-a-half-hour drive to Raleigh yet to go. Not encouraging when he was already wiped out from another long week in the rat race.

He grabbed his carry-on and his coat, then pushed into the line of passengers exiting the aircraft. He strode like clockwork down the Jetway and into the terminal. Time to get this show on the road.

Hurrying through the crowded terminal, Gaston decided to make a dash for the men's room while waiting for his luggage to arrive at the baggage claim. As he stood at the urinal, he stared at the blank wall, still pondering his predictable life. What was he doing here, in yet another sterile airport bathroom? How many times had he caught himself saying lately, "I can't wait for this day, this night, this week, this month to be over . . . I can't wait to get home . . . I can't wait to be happy"? He sighed as a face came to mind, a face from a happier time. He grinned as he pictured his grandmother Lois—the happiest person he had ever known.

Grandma Lois often visited Gaston's thoughts, especially when he was deep in regret. He could hear her now, telling him, "Don't wish your life away, Gaston . . ." She always seemed to have the right words for every occasion. In all her years in the classroom, Grandma Lois had watched so many of her students grow up, only to see them become trapped or disillusioned by the world's demands. Gaston knew she'd held onto better hopes for him.

Even though small in stature, Grandma Lois had been tall in wisdom—her mouth full of sagacious sayings that never failed to hit home. Considering she'd been around the block for some eighty-plus years before her passing, she knew a thing or two. And she had done her best to plant some of those seeds of wisdom along Gaston's path. Based on the way things were going in his life, though, perhaps he had strayed too far from that garden road. His life was definitely out of control . . . and he wondered how it would feel to stop himself dead in his tracks.

As he washed his hands, a headphone-wearing teenager hurried out the door and back into the airport. Gaston followed the kid with his eyes, then briefly glanced at his own face in the mirror. He immediately dropped his gaze before looking up again and wondering why the person looking back at him was unrecognizable.

Standing to his left at the double sink was a grey-suited, potbellied, balding gentleman. *Probably in his early sixties,* Gaston guessed, turning to appraise him further. But the man was staring straight at him.

The stranger tossed his head in the direction of the exit door. "Such a waste, huh? Throwin' his life away." Without waiting for a reply, he went on. "Kids these days . . . just wanderin' around, followin' dead-end roads." He tossed up a hand. "They have not a clue where they're headed, ya know?"

Gaston nodded in agreement, a right-tilting smirk on his face. The man dried his hands, then threw his brown paper towel in the trash before disappearing around the corner.

Gaston turned to the mirror for one last look. He slicked back a shock of unruly hair, then, pushing away the thoughts of what he had just seen, tossed away his own wad of paper, and darted out of the men's room.

He headed down the escalator to baggage claim. By the time he had chased down his luggage, he realized he badly needed coffee, an energy drink, *something* to keep him going on the long drive to Raleigh. But first, he needed a car.

"Good evening, sir. Welcome to Enterprise Rent-A-Car.

You must be Mr. Jones," said the small, dark-skinned, Hispanic woman standing behind the desk. All of five feet tall, she wore high heels, a beautiful blue-and-yellow dress with red stitching, and a glowing smile that lit up like a candle on a cold winter's night. *Maybe she's of the pecan pie–scented candle variety,* Gaston thought, *because she sure does smell good.* His stomach growled in appreciation.

"How did you know I was Mr. Jones?" he asked, looking down at his watch. "On top of that, how could you possibly have a smile on your face at 11:45 at night?"

"Well, first of all, we were expecting you, Mr. Jones. You're our last customer of the evening. Second, I love my job. I'm blessed to *have* a job. So many are dissatisfied, you know, searching for their passion in life—or more than that, their purpose."

She turned and pulled some paperwork from the printer. Gaston, reeling a bit from both fatigue and the unexpected observations of this petite philosopher, couldn't help but wonder if she had somehow been in touch with his now-deceased yet unforgotten Grandmother Lois.

"Here you are, Mr. Jones. Now if you'll just sign here..."

As Gaston looked over the papers, she went on. "As I was saying, I feel it's important to love what you do. If you're not happy with yourself and your work, life can be a drag, don't you think? Toxic and taxing. If you're full of toxins, unfortunately they can spill over and onto others, especially the people closest to you. Some folks just need a reality check. You know, the ones who are so focused on themselves that they can't see anything else in life? That's how I see it. So, I choose to be happy. Just like you . . . Right, Mr. Jones?"

Hello, sucker punch, he thought to himself. Even though he felt as low as a schoolboy being scolded by a teacher, he had to admit this woman had a point. "Of course, uh . . . Ms. Maria Londoño," he said, reading the name tag pinned to her dress. He blinked heavily. "Got to be happy, for sure. So important."

With his fidgety fingers in motion, he waited impatiently while she fetched the keys to the rental car. When she returned, she handed them over along with his completed paperwork. "Be safe, Mr. Jones," she said, smiling sweetly, as if he were her first and not her last customer of the day. "And thanks for allowing our team at Enterprise to serve you. Have blessed travels and a blessed rest of the week."

Gaston turned to walk away, feeling strangely as if he'd been delivered a message from heaven. *What does this angel have that I don't?* he wondered. *Why can't I have the kind of presence she has? Where do you get that kind of happiness, joy, and gratitude?*

Exiting the elevator to the right on parking garage level 2, Gaston saw that the only rental car left was his red, four-door Ford Taurus in parking spot A-18. As he pulled his luggage behind him, he was strongly tempted to jump in the car, lean back in the seat, and sleep until morning.

Instead, after loading his baggage into the trunk, he slid into the driver's seat, leaned his head and heavy heart on the steering wheel, and cried.

How had things spiraled so out of control? Why had he allowed himself to live a life of pretense and cover-up for so long? No one really knew him, or loved him, for that matter. No one except maybe Conner. But Conner loved everybody.

Gaston knew he had to get a grip—had to get this runaway railcar on the right track before he ran out of steam or, more importantly, time. He had faced inner turbulence before, but never like this. He sniffed and wiped his hands over his face. *Why do we allow ourselves to become what the world wants us to be?* he asked himself. *Did God create me for this?* At the thought, he sat up straighter. He realized he hadn't thought about God in a long time.

With a hurried shift in gears, he angled out of the parking slot, made a hard right, and pulled onto North Jackson Street. His eyes moved across the roadway, on the lookout for a convenience store. He had to get some caffeine in him—and quick.

Five minutes from the airport, he spotted a gas station—Bailey's Quick Mart Gas and Tote. It was not very modern or well lit, but it was open.

Near the front door, he pulled in beside the only vehicle in sight, a silver Honda Civic, '90s model, with a front quarter panel missing. At least one other human being was up at this hour, but so far he hadn't seen them. He got out of the car and went inside.

"Hello?" he called from just inside the sliding doors. "Anybody around?"

A tall, slender man of Indian descent appeared from out of nowhere, phone glued to his ear. "Yeah? You want something?"

"Coffee, please. If it's fresh."

"Made it about an hour and thirty ago." He gestured toward a large coffee machine on the back wall next to a cooking stand, where three big hot dogs stared back at him from their rolling shelf. *Now those might not be so fresh,* Gaston thought.

The coffee was no Juan Valdez Colombian Dark, but it was plenty strong. Gaston swallowed two-thirds of a cup of the steaming brew, then poured himself a refill for the road. He grabbed some peanut butter crackers and peanut M&M's, then made his way to the counter and held out a wrinkled twenty-dollar bill.

The timing couldn't have been more precise. No sooner had he put his $13.84 change in his pocket and turned to walk out the door than a heavy rain, mixed with sleet, began pelting the pavement. He pulled up the hood of his charcoal-grey Cabela's jacket and made a run for the car.

"I must be the luckiest guy in the world," he muttered, ducking into the car.

As he slammed the door, water dripped from his clothing onto the seat and the floor. He mopped at the moisture with his handkerchief, then opened up the midnight snack and sat as his car engine idled, still trying to warm up from an unseasonably cold thirty-three degrees. Taking a few minutes to thaw out, he sipped his coffee and nibbled on a stale cracker.

Wet, frustrated, and exhausted, he punched on the car radio and started surfing the stations. Might as well find some company to keep him awake on this stormy night. He finally tuned in to a program out of New Orleans called *Late Night with Crazy Eddie* on KWLT The Strike.

"If you're hanging out with me tonight," Eddie was saying, "we're going to cover the waterfront . . . I'm talkin' tropical storms, politics, religion—now, *there's* a couple topics designed to strike sparks—and y'all who know me know I don't mind a little controversy myself. But for the faint of heart, tonight we'll talk sports' biggest busts and the top ten things women want from men. So come on back right after the break."

Gaston couldn't care less about some of those topics, but he definitely needed to hear the last one, seeing as he was still single. He downed the last of the coffee, feeling a tiny surge of energy. One thing was for sure: He wasn't going to make it to Raleigh sitting still. Revving the engine, he turned the wipers on at full rotation, then eased out of the parking lot onto North Jackson so he could hit the exit ramp onto the interstate heading east.

Forty-five minutes into the drive, while burning the midnight oil on I-85, Gaston realized he didn't know where he was going. He peered around the dashboard to look for help, but there was no GPS in sight. Impatient, he used one hand to fish for the computer printout bearing the address of the hotel in

Raleigh where he'd be spending what was left of the night. When he didn't feel it on the seat, he opened the glove compartment. Not there either. *Must be on the floorboard,* he thought.

As he fumbled, leaning over to grab hold of the elusive paper, what he didn't see was a patch of ponding water that was icing over. All he would remember was the sound and sensation of metal on metal as the red Taurus slammed into the guardrail, then flipped over just before the whole world went black.

TWO

Sometimes you find yourself in the middle of nowhere.
Sometimes, in the middle of nowhere, you find yourself.
—Unknown

North Carolina State Trooper Brian Jennings's scanner was buzzing as he responded to a trucker's CB radio call. A mangled car had been spotted off the road, upside down, with smoke rushing from the hood. Officer Jennings felt that familiar dread as he turned on his flashing lights and sped toward the scene.

Being the first responder to accidents like this was an honor he wished on no one. Thankfully, moments after exiting his vehicle and running down the embankment, he heard the EMTs arriving behind him. As he clicked on his flashlight to peer inside, he saw the car was hardly recognizable—and not the only thing in bad condition. He found a male driver, unconscious, and an enormous amount of blood. Within moments the paramedics and firefighters were moving quickly and carefully around the car, working to keep the man alive—if only temporarily.

Soon the area was swarming with emergency personnel—more firefighters to clear the wreckage and troopers to direct the I-85 traffic. As he gasped for air and trudged up the rocky embankment, Officer Jennings remarked to another officer, "That man shouldn't have survived."

With shattered glass peeling back his facial skin, an unconscious Gaston Jones was transported to Moses H. Cone Memorial Hospital in Greensboro, North Carolina.

"Breathe! Come on . . . just breathe." Holding the patient's hand gently in both of hers, the tall, attractive ER nurse homed in on the beeping monitor. "Mr. Jones? Mr. Jones, can you hear me? My name is Anne Thomas, and I'm your nurse. I'm going to take good care of you . . . Can you hear me?" She was doing her best to offer a bit of hope, but despite her efforts, the spiral-haired blonde wondered if she was losing this patient. With the other medical personnel circling constantly, she closed her eyes, almost breathless. *This is serious,* she thought. With the man's hand in hers, she lifted up a silent prayer: *Please, God. I know the odds, but You can keep this man alive.* Anne's prayers for her patients reflected a heart that cared for strangers as if they were her own family—which is why she prayed for miracles.

She knew his odds were poor at best, and she wondered if Gaston Jones knew how little time he actually had. Staring down the seconds, she knew it wouldn't be long before he was gone—and there wasn't much more she could do. Every minute could mean the difference—because honestly, that might be all he had.

Miracles do happen. Gaston Jones spent some three weeks in the critical care unit in a medically induced coma, having many vivid dreams. Some dreams featured a kind face, a blonde-haired angel, whose caring touch and soothing voice seemed familiar and mysterious all at once.

The doctors and nurses were astonished at what happened next. After weeks of near lifelessness, Gaston awoke—and came face-to-face with what had saved his life.

THREE

We are people of purpose.
Are you living yours?
—Marlo Morgan

Gaston Jones seemed to have it all—or at least whatever "having it all" meant to an eight-year-old kid. He was born and raised on 317 Critz Street in a small town called Hernando, Mississippi, just outside of Memphis and barely across the state lines of both Tennessee and Arkansas. This cozy, quiet city was the place for which the great explorer Hernando de Soto was recognized after he discovered the Mississippi River in 1541.

In DeSoto County, life seemed great, and it was for most families. Everything is perfect when you don't know any better, and Gaston didn't. For the most part, he figured he would grow up and be like everybody else there in this easygoing, blue-collar town. Both his mom, Mattie Sue Jones, and his dad, Cully Ben Jones, had taught him about hard work through exemplary living—and about what mattered in life and what didn't.

Mattie, a Mississippi-born Southern belle, was a fourth-grade teacher at Carlisle Elementary, just five minutes from the house and across the street from what used to be the old Wilson Pleasure Park Skating Rink. Cully, born in East Texas in 1944, was a salesman, and a very good one at that—though his hat had changed in recent years due to unforeseen circumstances. He had become the president and CEO of Jones Insurance & Investments Group after his father, the late William Ben Jones, passed from a massive heart attack while on a fishing trip on the Barnett Reservoir with his best friend, Mr. Frank Lyles. Cully's father had started the family business in 1958, so it was natural that Cully would be next in line.

Over the years, Cully was a very involved and respected citizen in his community—president of the Rotary club, a Sunday school teacher at First United Methodist Church, Habitat for Humanity co-chair, acting vice president of the Boys & Girls Club, and of course, Little League baseball coach for Gaston's team. Mattie and Cully were determined to raise Gaston in a way that taught respect for others. He learned to say "Yes, ma'am" and "Yes, sir" to his elders, to help the less fortunate, to be grateful for what he had, to do things the right way, to have his priorities in order, and to stand up for what he believed in.

A sense of pride was very prevalent throughout the community, and for good reason. Mattie and Cully were grateful to be raising the next generation in Hernando.

❖

When it came to common sense, young Gaston had plenty. He often spoke to anyone who would listen about his dreams and his perspective on life. Among his goals was the hope of one day meeting Dr. William R. Sheads—his greatest hero besides his dad. Dr. Sheads had established the prestigious SHEADS Award to be presented to a citizen worthy of recognition for great contribution to his or her community. Also at the top of his goals was becoming a successful businessman like his dad and late grandfather—only, of course, if a professional sports career didn't work out.

Like most little boys, Gaston also shared the wish of one day having a baby brother. He imagined himself and a brother playing sports together, camping together, wrestling together, and growing up and sharing life experiences, like most of his friends with brothers seemed to be doing.

Unfortunately, an unwelcome prognosis stood in the way of that dream. His mother shared with Gaston when he was five years old that, because of a health condition her doctor had found, his baby-brother wish would never be possible. A tough and deflating conversation, to say the least, and with no say-so in the matter, a dejected young Gaston threw a fit—along with a few toys—as he stormed to his room, slammed the door, and lay across his bed, staring at his collection of sports memorabilia.

❖

It was a bright mid-May Saturday morning, and George Evans was already busily engaged at his place of business, Evans's Shoe Shine Parlor. He knew that on such a fine morning, he could likely expect a visit from his good friend Cully Jones, as he did on most Saturdays after breakfast. Mr. Jones would probably bring his son, too, if nothing of importance needed to be done around their house. Cully and George had been friends for many years in this small Hernando community, where George and his family had settled after he'd served his country for some twenty years and then traveled the country in his Rabbit Foot Blues Band.

There was a shop called Thompson Shoe Repair when Evans arrived in town, located at 415 Main Street near Brewer's Bakery, Prince's Family Drug Store, and the First Smith Bank. It was owned by Mr. Dick "Pops" Thompson and his wife, Kats. George began working there when Pops had only one chair in the corner for shining shoes.

In the summer of 1969, Pops Thompson decided to sell and move to New Orleans, and it was then that George Evans chose to buy him out. Practically six months after the takeover, Mr. Evans decided to move just around the corner in the adjoining and vacated old Robert B. Adcock's Barbershop building on 538 Marcel Crockett Avenue. This was where a shining legacy of impacting lives began.

The original Evans's Shine Parlor that was established on January 17, 1970, had actually been in the works long before he took ownership. Through all his hardships, shortfalls, and other adverse situations, George had been constructing his dream for a long time, not only in his head and heart, but also with pen and paper. Matter of fact, on an old, yellow sheet of paper from a notepad he'd found in his Grandpa Jesse Carver's nightstand. The page outlined the goals and dreams he had inked up some twenty years earlier. It was a little faded now, but not far removed from his successful blueprint. He had known early on the footprint he wanted to leave behind, yet more than that, he knew what was expected of him. He would not only be a difference maker in the community where his roots lay, but also in the lives of the young people he would impact for many years to come.

George Evans had grown up in difficult times. As a young black boy in the South, he had experienced how "equality" was not equal at all. His grandmother had always taught him that every man and woman should be treated the same, no matter their color—but he knew that wasn't the way people always behaved. A "spade" was not a spade! He vowed to himself and to his grandmother that one day he would have his own business, and when he did, he would show the world from the streets he traveled and the paths he crossed that everyone was important—beginning in DeSoto County. He knew it would be a challenge, but he was determined that fairness be the rule and not the exception. Also, that respect would be both given and earned. He would expect the best from those who chose to patronize his business, and he would provide it in return. His customers—black, white, or brown—

would be treated as if they and their families were the most important people in the world that particular day—because they were! George Evans wanted them to feel that their dollar was well spent, and that serving them was an honor for him, not an obligation.

During segregation, the barbershops typically had two chairs for whites and one for blacks—on opposite sides of the room from each other, of course. Until . . . well, until times changed. *Everybody* in George's shop was treated with dignity, unlike the disrespect his late Grandpa Jesse had experienced. The days of integration had been difficult ones. George remembered when the white people would drive by the shop to see if any blacks were there, and the black people would drive by to see if any white people were in the shop. The memories had never left young George's mind. He had seen and breathed them for far too long—but he knew that one day he would not carry life's scuffs with him as pain, but as seeds for a solution. Without exception, that was just the way it was going to be! Forgiveness was part of healing, and a necessary step toward reconciliation for the future. He didn't say any of this out loud, but he lived it. And if you worked for Mr. Evans, you "got" it.

A few years and fifteen chairs later, there were no "sides"—just a preferred choice for seating. Each man or woman was welcomed at the door with a greeting, a friendly smile, a look in the eye, and a firm handshake. George Evans would have it no other way. Polished in his faith and beliefs, he soon began influencing customers from the surrounding states—Tennessee, Louisiana,

Arkansas, Missouri—as people drove many miles out of their way to experience the simple, engaging, and therapeutic culture he had created. George Evans's shop not only demonstrated how the world should be, but also how it *would* be.

Every kind of person—from doctors, to engineers, to career military personnel, firemen, musicians, educators, politicians, and even professional athletes—patronized Evans's Shoe Shine Parlor. It was the kind of place you wanted to visit every week, and for good reason. Medicine for the soul. You just felt better about yourself and life when you left. Over the years, people around town discovered that more than any pair of shoes, *lives* got cleaned up at the shoe shine parlor. A little shine went a long way! Matter of fact, every time a customer would leave, one of the store employees would say, "Shine on!"—and it was customary for the customer to repeat the phrase before walking out the door. Fortunately for Cully Jones, Mr. Evans had been "shining on" for many years, and now his wisdom was beginning to trickle down to young Gaston's heart.

"Welcome and good morning, Mr. Jones. It is so good to see you. How may I serve you today?" said Rogerick, the slender thirteen-year-old black boy who had been working at the shoe shop for a little over a year and a half. Mr. Evans only hired young black boys ranging from ages nine to eighteen. He hoped he could be a father figure to them and positively impact the way they saw the future, since most of them came from homes without a father, or at least a constructive one. Some had a man in the house, but sadly enough, these men were just as absent in their own right as any absentee father.

Even though at least a dozen boys were employed there at any given time, Mr. Evans gave his hired hands little slack. Instead he gave them life lessons so they could learn how life should look. Pride overcame him as he watched each of the boys endeavoring to become a purposeful young man who respected and selflessly served others. He buffed and polished their lives so they, too, could put a shine on the lives of the customers who came through the doors on Marcel Crockett Avenue. Sometimes a few of the boys didn't always see eye to eye with Mr. Evans, even though they always looked him there. But they knew he had their best interests at heart, and he would take care of them, love them, and help them anytime he could, whether inside or outside the shop. Many times he drove them home after work, bought them a bite of supper, or did things to help their families. He even picked them up on Sundays to take them to church if they had no ride.

Over time, many of Evans's young men would become the spitting image of his own character: knowing how to treat people, understanding what honesty really meant, respecting others, keeping their word, and serving their fellow man with gratitude. Some boys became the first person in their families to ever attend college, own a home, and make a name for themselves.

Before Cully could respond to Rogerick, he and his son received another warm welcome. "Good morning, Mr. Jones. Who you got with you, sir?" Mr. Evans hollered to his good friend from the back of the store. He most always stood or sat there, busily cleaning behind the many racks and shelves of shoes, boots, socks, shoe polish, brushes, belts, and other leather goods. Sometimes he just stayed there to monitor his hired boys from a distance. Even if you never saw Mr. Evans, you always heard him or knew he was there. He never missed a moment to share what was on his mind and give you "a piece of it" if needed.

Yet again, before Mr. Jones could answer, Evans continued. "Rogerick," he said loudly, "did you ask Mr. Jones about his family? Did you introduce yourself to his son? Did you offer him a newspaper or something to drink? You know better! Make sure you make notes of all personal information Mr. Jones gives you in your client file and in the one between your ears. That way, next time he comes in, you will remember how to greet him. Nothing less, Rock!"

"Yes, sir," responded the young boy, now embarrassed. He sighed and rested his chin on his chest. When he raised his head, he saw the boy who had entered with Mr. Jones peering at him. Rogerick guessed they were close to the same age. "What's your name?" he asked.

"I'm Gaston . . . Jones, of course." The boy had a friendly smile.

"Gaston," Rogerick said, "you got any brothers or sisters?"

Gaston didn't really know how to respond. Rogerick led them to two chairs, where Gaston sat beside his dad and watched as the boy began to wipe a tan cloth back and forth across the top of his dad's shoe. Caught off guard by the boy's question, Gaston had gone quiet and dropped his gaze when the boy had asked. *Brothers or sisters?* He was already sensitive to the topic, so how would he answer? He decided the best answer was no answer, so he turned and glanced out the front window, his eyes following the Little Debbie bread truck passing by.

Cully glanced at his son and decided to speak up for him. "He sure wants one real bad. Not sure God has it in His plans for us, though, Rogerick." He sighed, then added, "We're not exactly sure what the future holds, but we know God holds our future."

"Yes, sir, Mr. Jones. I understand that," Rogerick said. Gaston wondered if Rogerick had sensed the tense silence in the air.

About that time the door chimed as another local walked in and changed the subject—and Gaston was glad for that.

A chirping noise sounded as Mattie Jones walked through the front door of the Women's Clinic of Hernando, some three blocks off the downtown square on Teryl Stennis Drive. It couldn't have been a prettier day—a very comfortable Tuesday afternoon in October. Apparently the autumn leaves were not the only things changing at this time of year. Mattie was pregnant—thirteen weeks pregnant, to be exact.

If truth be told, she and Cully were somewhat apprehensive. They had been down this road before. Carrying Gaston had been difficult for Mattie, who'd suffered from preeclampsia, polycystic ovarian syndrome, severe nausea, and sleep deprivation. Not to mention, they had lost a child at twenty-four weeks, some three years after Gaston was born. So, though these were not uncharted waters, they were nerve-racking, to say the least.

A close friend of hers had endured five miscarriages before having her first child. Mattie had done all she could to try and avoid that, yet she knew the ultimate outcome was out of their hands. She could only do the best with what she knew, let the process be the process, and refuse to focus on any negative thoughts.

A slight knock on the door signaled the entry of Mattie's obstetrician, Dr. Barbara Ann Minchew. Taking a seat on the nearby four-legged rolling stool, she handed Mattie three sheets of paper. The first two pages were the results of her bloodwork, progress charts, and a brief overview of what the numbers meant. The last page included two ultrasound images of her and Cully's unborn "miracle"

baby. What medically never was supposed to have happened... *had* happened.

Then Dr. Minchew delivered the unfathomable news.

FOUR

You are not an accident! Even before the universe was created,
God . . . planned you for his purposes. These purposes will
extend far beyond the few years you will spend on earth.
—Rick Warren

Suddenly, the cushionless white wooden chair felt twice as hard as it had a moment ago. "Our baby has . . . what?" she said, almost in a whisper.

Dr. Minchew reached for her hand and calmly repeated, "Well, Mattie, we're not entirely certain. Your bloodwork has some hormonal indicators that could mean any number of things. Down syndrome is just one of those possibilities."

Disbelief raced through Mattie's head. "This cannot be happening . . ." She placed her other hand on her stomach, imagining the baby inside her—and the range of outcomes awaiting her family. As a schoolteacher, she knew the statistics: that about six thousand babies were born in the United States every year with an extra chromosome. *But why us?* she thought. *Why me?* She and Cully were still young parents by most standards. They didn't match the profile of Down parents.

Dr. Minchew continued to stroke Mattie's shaking

hand. "Please understand, Mattie, that we will do whatever we can to take care of your baby—no matter the diagnosis. If Down syndrome is what you're facing, your child will have so much love to give," she continued, smiling gently. "Perfection comes in all shapes and sizes. And did I forget to mention that it's a boy?"

❖

Driving home, Mattie began to pray, to cast her cares on the Lord, and to pour out her heart in an effort to gain some measure of peace. Amazingly, her stomach began to unknot, and the fear and pain slowly trickled away, to be replaced with . . . What was that she was feeling? Gratitude? Yes. Not one to live in denial, she resolved to embrace the truth: She and Cully had been chosen to take care for a special child with an uncertain future. They had wanted a baby, and that prayer had been answered—and no matter what lay ahead for their son and their family, she would pray over him until her dying breath. For now, she would pray for a strong, vigorous little boy. And if he happened to have an extra chromosome, so be it.

What she couldn't have known was how that "extra one," that one extra chromosome, would eventually change the world . . . at least the world she lived in.

❖

When Cully answered the phone on the third ring, he was surprised to hear Mattie on the other end.

"Honey," she said, "do you have a few minutes to meet me at the Coffee Beanery? I know you are busy, but I just wanted a few minutes with you."

Cully knew she had been at the doctor's office for her periodic checkup. He noticed that at least she sounded calm. "Is the baby okay?" he asked immediately.

"Baby's fine," she said. "Strong heartbeat."

So why did he have this strange premonition, as if maybe things were not so great?

"For sure," he said. "Be there in a minute."

He would never forget pulling into the parking lot right off Jefferson Street and into a marked space right next to hers. His grey 1974 Volkswagen "Happy Van" with a red pinstripe down the side was his "running around town" vehicle of choice. He had lovingly named this van Jorgito ("Little George" in Spanish) after the old, beat-up truck from the bilingual cartoon *Thundering George* that Gaston had watched as a preschooler.

The sunlight ricocheted off the lightly tinted driver's side glass as he watched his beautiful wife step out of her new, burgundy four-door Honda Accord LX and open the rickety van door. When she got in, he was taken aback. "Aren't we going in?" he asked, nodding toward the coffee shop.

Mattie didn't answer, but instead tugged the rickety door shut, then turned and gave him a wholesome smile before leaning over and kissing him gently on the cheek.

"What was *that* for?" he said, a grin forming on his

face. And yet ... why did he get the feeling something was wrong?

Again she didn't answer, but instead turned to face the front window and stared out, as if trying to gather her words. When she finally spoke, her words left Cully speechless. He felt as though he had been knocked to the floor by Mike Tyson.

"Cully, there's something wrong with our baby. The doctor mentioned a few possible diagnoses, but it's very possible that our son has Down syndrome."

The words *our son* registered in Cully's mind, but he was still too overwhelmed to speak. Before he could say another word, Mattie went on. "But listen, I am saying this from the bottom of my heart: There is *beauty in the unexpected*, and as long as this baby lives, we are gonna love him just like we do Gaston. No matter how scared or uncertain we're feeling right now"—her voice cracked, and she stopped to take a deep breath—"this little boy will be a blessing to us and the joy of our hearts."

Mattie repeated everything she'd learned from the doctor—the results of her bloodwork, the possibilities of abnormalities, and the chances of her miscarrying or worse. Paralyzed, Cully just sat there with his mouth wide open as the radio played, unheard, some Whitney Houston song.

At long last, Mattie reached over to turn off the radio. "Cully, everything is going to be okay. My being pregnant is already a miracle, and I'm going to pray for this baby to have a long and healthy life. Gaston always dreamed of a brother ... and I believe God has answered his prayer."

With a tortured look on his face, an emotionally charged Cully answered, "Yes, but is *this* what Gaston dreamed of? It's not what *I* dreamed of! What if I'll never be able to throw baseballs or footballs with him, shoot baskets, or... Even if he lives, will he be able to do normal kid stuff?" He shook his head from side to side. "This is just not the way I imagined it."

For what seemed like an hour, silence filled the van as a whirlwind of emotions swirled in Cully's mind: shock, sadness, anger, self-pity, but then, at last, remorse. Had he not even *thought* about how Mattie must be feeling?

Ashamed of himself, Cully turned to Mattie and grasped her hand. "Matts, I'm sorry!"

She didn't look at him—just kept staring out the window.

"Please forgive me," he went on. "Will you? We *will* love him—dearly."

And he meant it.

Complete silence! Cully sat wondering if maybe his parents had felt similarly when they'd found out he was a redheaded boy instead of a blonde, blue-eyed girl. Maybe even their unborn son would not have chosen Cully if he'd had a vote.

Cully hadn't asked to be dealt this risky hand, but as he steeled himself, a thought, unbidden, came to his mind. He would be an *intentional* father, the kind of man his good friend George Evans was trying to teach his young employees to be when they grew up. He would pray for his son before he came into the world, and if God granted them a future, he would instill in his son the many great traits that George preached about and modeled. And <u>he would embrace the challenge of uncertainty</u> and <u>cherish every moment ahead</u>. He took a deep breath of resolve and gave Mattie's hand a playful little jiggle. She finally turned to look at him.

"I'm ready," he said. He smiled as tears of happiness—and relief—streamed down her face.

❖

It couldn't have been a better Saturday. The kitchen stove clock read exactly 11:11 on this beautiful, hot, and unseasonably humid October morning as Mattie leaned out of the back porch screen door. "Gaston, will you please come inside for a minute?" she called. "Daddy has got something to talk to you about. And grab some grape Gatorade from the refrigerator. You look hot."

Gaston came tearing in, his football thudding to the floor as he headed toward the kitchen cabinets. He grabbed a plastic St. Louis Cardinals cup out of the cupboard, then snatched the grape Gatorade—his favorite—out of the fridge and filled his cup full. He took a big swig, downing about half of the cup, then stomped into the living room. He plopped down on the couch to play with Tater and Socks, his dog and cat who—amazingly—got along.

Thump, thump, thump, down the wooden staircase Dad came. He patted Gaston on the head as he passed into the kitchen to grab a glass of freshly made sweet tea. He returned a moment later and sat down across from Gaston in his brown leather recliner—last year's Christmas gift from the Jimmy Harrison family. Mattie sat down beside Gaston on the couch and shooed Tater and Socks away.

It was not uncommon for the Jones family to sit down together and have family discussions in the living room, yet this time something seemed different to Gaston.

"Son, Mommy and Daddy have a pretty neat secret to share with you," Mattie said.

Am I getting a new bike? he wondered. *Or is Dad finally going to build me a treehouse?*

"Gaston, what is the one thing you have always wanted here at the house?" Mom asked with a grin on her face.

Well, he'd always wanted to grow up and be a professional basketball player . . . oh, but wait. Mom had said "here at the house." He looked from one parent to the other for some indication as he racked his brain to come up with the right answer.

"Well, guess what, Gaston?" said Cully.

"What, Dad?"

"Mommy is pregnant, and you are going to have what you've always wanted—a baby brother!"

"Holy cow!" shouted Gaston ecstatically. He jumped off the couch, spilling what was left of his Gatorade. Screaming with happiness and running around the room as if he had just won the Little League World Series, he scared Tater and Socks so badly that they dashed out of the room and hid.

When at last he wound down, he joined his parents for a big family hug.

By now, tears were streaming down his parents' faces.

"But, Mommy," said Gaston, breathing hard, "I thought you said I wouldn't ever have a baby brother."

"Yes, Gaston. That is what the doctor had told me," she said. "But we put the final decision in God's hands and just trusted Him. And we'll have to trust God even more because, well . . . the doctor said your brother might be sick when he gets here, or he might be a little different. But we don't need to worry about that today. God is making you a big brother—and you're going to be a great one at that. Isn't that the coolest news you have ever heard?"

Gaston looked puzzled. "What do you mean, Mommy? Why would the baby be sick?"

"Hopefully the baby will be happy and healthy, so we're going to pray for God to take care of him. Can you pray for him too?"

"Yes, Mom. I'm sooooo excited! When will he be here?"

"Well, in a few months. The first week in March," she said.

"That's what I'm talking about! Oh, Mom, you just don't know . . . This is all I've ever wanted! Can I go tell the good news to my friends—to Kirby and Brad and T. C. and Trey and Todd and Nanna Hutch and—"

His mother cut him off. "Yes, Gaston," she said, laughing, with tears still welling in her eyes. "Go!"

Big brother. Oh, that sounded so good! And that's what he was going to be. He had no idea that his little brother would be born with Down syndrome, but it wouldn't have mattered to him anyway.

❖

On Thursday, April 15, 1976, the baby arrived, and Gaston was beside himself with joy. Kissing the tiny forehead over and over and over again, he was amazed and moved to tears. He had just laid eyes for the first time on his baby brother—Conner Dale Jones. Who could *not* love him and kiss him?

Little Conner lay quietly next to his mother on the hospital bed, wearing a baby blue shirt that read, "Life is good—enjoy the ride!" On the shirt was a picture of a little boy riding a bicycle with training wheels.

Gaston never could have known that, though his training wheels had come off, Conner's never would. But even more, he never would have guessed the impact that this little baby would one day have on his own life—a life that would be forever changed by this tiny "extra one."

FIVE

Make sure the outside of you is a good reflection
of the inside of you.
—Jim Rohn

The day couldn't have taken any longer to arrive. Gaston had been excited all week—all month, for that matter—in anticipation of "The Greatest Show on Earth" coming to town, and time had slowed to a molasses crawl. Actually, the circus was coming to Memphis, but that was only some twenty minutes or so away and a few miles north across the state line. Conner was at home with Dad, and Mom had checked Gaston out of school early that Thursday to give the two of them plenty of extra time to beat the sold-out crowd. Everything stopped when the circus came to town—or, at least, everything stopped in Gaston's mind. He had been five years in a row—almost as far back as he could remember.

As they parked and headed toward the ticket gates, Gaston's smile stretched from ear to ear. He could only imagine what was to come. What would he enjoy the most? The pink and blue cotton candy, the mammoth-sized elephants, the roaring Bengal tigers, or the candy apple red–nosed clowns and their outlandish outfits? The clowns never failed to entertain, dressed up in stylistic colorful attire, huge shoes, and decorative makeup with painted-on smiles. They were full of surprises, running in and out of the arena to make people laugh before disappearing for good. It was truly a sight to behold.

Since his first visit to the circus as a little boy, Gaston had acquired a passion for clowning. He became a "wannabe" performer after falling in love with the complexities a few simple grease paints could create on a face, and sometimes he daydreamed about joining the circus and traveling the world as a clown. He presumed that anyone with sense would dream about making people laugh every day. By the way the clowns acted, Gaston supposed theirs was the most fun job in the whole world.

That night at the circus was as magical as any other. As he ate from his own bag of buttery popcorn, Gaston marveled at the acrobats and the graceful prancing horses—but he especially loved the orange-haired clown who laughed, cried, fell down, stood up again, and entertained the rapt crowd. Gaston loved that he never knew what a clown was going to do next—but he *did* know that a clown's antics would not fail to make him smile. As he took in the sights and sounds of the show, he tapped his feet together beneath his seat, enjoying the soft thud of plastic from the pair of red clown shoes his mother had bought for him on the way inside the tent.

After coming home from another great night under the Big Top, Gaston sat on his bed with his oversized, clumsy clown shoes hanging over the edge. He looked down at the journal he held in his hands, wondering how to possibly describe the wonderful night he'd just had. *How in the world do people fill these shoes?* he thought. *They're just so big... too big to fill, in my opinion!*

As the clock struck 10:39 p.m., he finally put his pencil to paper. He wrote about his future life as a circus clown, as well as the burning questions he had about traveling with the circus. *What will I eat for dinner? Who will be my friends? Will I get to ride the horses, or even the elephants?* As he paged through the souvenir program he'd brought home and the copies he'd saved from previous years, he began to envision a fuller chapter, or even an entire book, in his mind. At the top of one page, he wrote, "My Story: A Clown's..." What should he call it? A clown's world? A clown's journey? He decided to save the title for later, for the time when he knew exactly what his story was going to be. For now, he would just write about the clown he'd seen tonight. And so, he began...

> The clown at the circus tonight was so funny! He didn't use words, but through his actions, he made me laugh. His love for putting on a show made me happy too. And then he walked away, slipped out... was gone without notice! *Who is that person?* I wondered. *Really?* I do wonder what that clown is like without his makeup, after the show. But I must admit he sure looked happy. He smiled a lot, and boy did I laugh.

It almost felt like I already knew him because he was just so funny like me. He didn't use words, but he made me laugh anyway. After the show, I got to talk to him for a few minutes. How lucky am I! When I asked him if he got tired of being in a traveling show, seeing new places every day, he said, "You don't really think about it. On and off the train you go . . . just unloading, performing, and loading up again every day or so, not knowing what city you are in or where you are going next. You just go. And when you get there, you really don't know where 'there' is." What a life!

Clowns wear colorful wigs and make-up, outlandish costumes, and funny, large footwear. (Mom bought some clown shoes for me to wear!) Clowns don't do what actors in plays do, pretending that the audience isn't in front of them. I like that clowns look at the audience. I also like that a clown can make you laugh in all kinds of ways—silly faces, gags, falls . . . It's a special kind of comedy.

I read in a book that clowns have been around forever—as far back as Ancient Egypt! But back then, they called their clowns "fools." Most of their clowns were born with something different about them, so they were usually the butt of the joke. They didn't decide to become clowns—they just had to be. That kind of clown would not be funny to me.

Today, there are many types of clowns. I especially love the character clowns. Some pretend to be serious clowns, and when they try to be tough, they fall on their faces and make the audience laugh. Other clowns pretend to be bossy know-it-alls. They always try to prove how smart they are—but the audience knows better.

Ever seen the ringmaster clown? He has to keep everyone happy by making sure everything looks as though it is going well or in the right direction. It's funny to watch him try so hard when everything is obviously a mess. What about the rodeo clown, who tries to make everyone laugh while running away from the beast at the same time? Now, *that's* entertaining to watch!

I bet their costumes can be uncomfortable. Their shoes are awkward, their costumes are heavy, their funny wigs are itchy . . . not to mention their makeup! They sure work hard to put on a good show for us. I might even call clowns my heroes. I can only imagine when I grow up what it will be like to be a—

Tap tap tap.
Gaston sat up straight at the sound of a few knocks

on his door. "Gaston, son, it is time to turn off your lights and go to bed," said his mom. "You have school tomorrow. We had fun tonight, but you need your rest to face another day of great opportunities!" She spoke gently from behind Gaston's nearly closed bedroom door.

Saddened to stop right in the middle of what he thought was a pretty good writing session, he said, "Yes, ma'am," and folded up his book. As he turned down his bed and clicked off the light, he grinned and told himself the remaining chapters could wait for another day. He was definitely dreaming up a brilliant plan.

❖

Gaston's other love was playing ball. He loved it and was unquestionably good at it. Playing sports was a constant friend, and Gaston learned to rely on the joy a good game could bring. He could lean on that predictability even during the toughest of times—and his family recognized his God-given athletic ability when he was very young. If he could bounce it, kick it, throw it, or hit it, Gaston was interested.

He learned so many things from playing sports—that is, when he paid attention to the lessons being taught. He practiced every day and was rewarded with name recognition, trophies, and championships. Besides the achievements, he learned life skills such as communication, teamwork, sportsmanship, dealing with losing and winning, and more than anything, playing with and respecting others.

But playing sports was not a one-man activity for Gaston. Despite the almost nine-year age gap between them, Gaston and Conner became best friends as Conner grew—and playing sports was one of the many things they did together. Even though Gaston's skill level was superior, it didn't bother Conner as long as he got to be with his hero, his big brother. Whether they kicked a ball in the backyard or loaded hooks to dunk in the family pond, they loved each other's company. Conner was an affectionate little boy who always made time for a hug—and usually two or three. More importantly, he was quick to tell his brother how much he meant to him, how much he loved him, and how special he was. He couldn't have been more proud of his big brother, Gaston.

"Beegee, y-you . . . ya know I luv ya, right? I'm very proud of ya, Beegee. Y-you know I am . . . alwades."

As a baby learning to speak, Conner referred to his brother as "Beegee"—his own version of Gaston's family nickname, "Big G." Conner loved everybody in such a unique, unconditional way that his presence was a breath of fresh air to anyone who knew him. Who couldn't love Conner? In his mind, he never met a stranger.

As the years went on, he didn't always talk a lot—but the words he said were careful and meaningful. He showed people he loved them through his actions, and he loved life and treated it like a gift. Conner often struggled to get his words out the way he wanted to, and some people never accepted his differences—but Conner carried on. He successfully climbed over every obstacle the world put in his way.

Meanwhile, Gaston faced the kinds of challenges many people never acknowledge—the quieter, subtler challenges of the heart.

❖

Gaston's double-striped socks and hiking clothes were a muddy mess. Michael Jackson's "Man in the Mirror" shook Gaston's boom box as he tossed his last stitch of dirty clothing, a wadded-up pair of underwear, at a mounting pile of laundry. Caught up in the melody, he streaked exuberantly toward the hot water running in his shower. He sang along at the top of his lungs, the words echoing around the now steaming hall shower. *How could life be any better?* he thought to himself. For the last three days he had been fishing, riding bikes, cooking out, and spending quality time with his best friend, Fisher Southerland, on Sardis Lake.

The only exception had been one moment of pure humiliation—when he'd wet the camper bed he shared with his friend on Friday night. Gaston's was a very embarrassing problem, and he had been dealing with it for a while—yet this time, he was unable to hide it. No one was supposed to know about it, but now ... they did. He couldn't cover this one up! When packing for her son's trip, Mattie had forgotten to toss in his prescription bottle; and after Gaston told her about the accident, she apologized profusely. She couldn't imagine the grief she had caused her oldest boy and vowed it would never, ever happen again.

Yet Gaston always seemed able to move forward with life's challenges pretty well, and by that evening, he had tried to put it all behind him. As he sang to himself in the shower, he looked down at the blotches of reddish skin that ran up his right arm, all the way up to his neck. Usually the redness—what some called "port-wine stains"—were easily concealed by Gaston's clothing. But not so tonight, as Gaston ran a bar of soap over the patch of red. Every time he caught a glimpse of the blotches, he was grateful they weren't in a more noticeable place.

Even when things weren't going his way, the skinny, happy-go-lucky Gaston sure knew how to make it seem as if he was on top of the world. At school he was voted Class Favorite and Best Dressed, even among the hecklers (including the jocks). Well liked, he was all about a good time and laughter—unless it came at his expense.

"Wasn't it fun, Gaston?" asked Mattie as she handed him a towel.

"Of course, Mother. But why does fun like that ever have to come to an end?" replied Gaston, a big smile painted on his young face.

As the family camped out around the dinner table, all eyes and ears were on Gaston. They happily listened as he recounted every detail of the weekend he had just spent with his bestie, Fisher. Just like Gaston and Conner, the two friends were inseparable. They had grown up playing T-ball together with Fisher's mom as the coach. Even though Fisher had moved some three and a half hours away for a few years due to his dad's work, he and Gaston had remained friends. And thankfully, this past January, the Southerland family had moved back to town.

After unloading his weekend agenda, brushing his teeth, and getting ready for bed, Gaston swallowed his pill and hit the pillow. School would come early tomorrow.

❖

As the sun broke the darkness Wednesday morning, Gaston awoke to find his mom and dad by his side. Barely alert, he sat up and yawned, rubbing his eyes as he stared at the clock. What were his parents doing there, and why they were both looking at him with such focus? It was definitely still way too early for school. Had he done something wrong?

His mind raced, and he remembered that he and Fisher had run past a No Trespassing sign over the weekend. Together they had sneaked through the tall grass to catch a few bass in a nearby private pond. Was it possible they were in trouble for *that*?

Mattie began to gently rub Gaston's cheek, and Cully's right hand landed on his son's left knee. He held a cup of water in the other, and before setting it aside on the nearby nightstand, he took a quick sip. Cully lightly cleared his throat, Mattie began to cry. Cully put his arm around Gaston.

"Big G, we've got to tell you something ... Yesterday ..."

He paused for what seemed like an hour. "Yesterday Fisher was riding his bike down the sidewalk in his neighborhood. He tried to cross the street toward the Handy Mart, but . . . I'm so sorry, but he was called home."

Gaston was bewildered. What was his dad trying to say? "Who called him home? What do you mean, he was called home?"

Choking up, Cully said, "Fisher was hit by a speeding car that didn't see him, and he went home to be with our Lord."

Gaston felt both stunned and empty. It took a moment for the words to register, and he began to shake. Gaston's face turned colors as he screamed.

SIX

*In the middle of difficulty
lies opportunity.
—Albert Einstein*

Gaston could not understand why this had happened to his most trusted friend, the person who knew everything about him. After Fisher's death, Gaston's insecurities took on new meaning. Afraid others might learn about his bedwetting secret, he stopped spending the night with friends. To make sure no one saw his blotchy, red skin, he began wearing two shirts and even warm-ups under his blue jeans. Everything felt like an embarrassment to him. He felt skinnier than ever and humiliated by every little joke. What once were minor difficulties had set up camp in a major way. Gaston's heart was forever changed.

❖

Though the hurt remained, Gaston sought ways to distract himself—and others—from the wounds within. He thought often of the clowns he'd so admired, tricksters who could distract a crowd with a well-timed gag or joke. Eventually, with the help of films, books, and juggling sessions, Gaston picked up his own type of clowning pretty quickly.

Whether for Halloween or a school play, Gaston chose to dress as his clown heroes whenever a costume was in order. His favorite was the "Auguste"—the most famous clown of all time. The Auguste clown was all about exaggeration, which Gaston mimicked perfectly. Of course he also admired the Joseph Grimali clown—the "whiteface" clown so many have come to know and love. No matter their methods, the different clowns managed to accomplish the same thing: to put on a convincing show for a rapt and willing audience.

Unfortunately, as Gaston grew older, he became all too familiar with the personal habit of covering up. Between the weight of the loss he experienced and the self-disgust he felt, he lacked confidence and the tools required to recover from his grief. Despite his attempts to play the willing fool, he found himself being laughed at—and not in the way of his choosing. There was not a tent big enough to hide what Gaston was feeling inside.

Before long, his everyday decisions began to direct his course toward a destination he never would have guessed. Gaston felt attacked from the inside and out—not only from his personal turbulence, but also from those who teased and prodded him. As he perfected his performance, Gaston realized that his show was working—and that the mask he wore was effectively covering his sadness and shame. Once seemingly an unshakeable kid, he now wondered if he could ever *not* be a clown. Wasn't it so much easier to pretend? To entertain?

SEVEN

*Every day that slips away is a day that
can never be retrieved.
—Steven K. Scott*

It was the spring of 1980—and no one could have foreseen the tragedy that lay ahead. Cully Jones knew something felt... well, not right. He just wasn't waking up the way he always did. Early each morning, usually around five a.m., he started his morning routine: a pot of coffee, a Smith's donut, some soul-searching quiet time, and then the morning news. One morning he noticed himself feeling more thirsty than usual. The coffee tasted as good as it always did, but he drank as if he had just played three sets of tennis on a hot summer day.

This continued for some time, and as the days and weeks went on, he started noticing some sensitive spots on his head. They weren't that big, but the spots quickly became knots. Always a jokester, Cully made light of the knots and let his golfing buddies at the DeSoto County Country Club call him "Old Hardhead" or "Knot Head"—appropriate nicknames considering his stubbornness. Many laughs were had at Cully's expense until those knots took on a new meaning.

For reasons he didn't know, Cully always felt exhausted and couldn't seem to get enough sleep. He would wake up three or four times in the middle of the night and struggle to go back to sleep. Waking up and staring at the ceiling for hours a night became all too common for Cully.

After a couple months of abnormal patterns, he decided to make an appointment with the local general practitioner in Hernando. "Good morning, Dr. Moore," said Cully, who waited in the examination room with Mattie.

"What brings you here today, Cully?" said Dr. Moore.

"Not sure, to be honest. But something just doesn't seem right, Doc. You know I have my morning routine—getting up at five when I am not on the road, having my cup of coffee and donut, enjoying some quiet time . . . Well, for a while now I have just been tired. On top of that, I'm always thirsty and have some little bumps on my head, especially right here on the top left side. Of course, all my buddies at the country club joke and say I'm just hardheaded, but . . . I am just not so sure that's it. I know I can be a stubborn mule sometimes, but what if this is something else? So, I figured I would come see what this is all about. Mattie has been on me about this for some time now too." He turned toward his wife and squeezed her hand.

Looking at him with a kind smile, Dr. Moore said, "Well, let's take a look and see if we can find out what is going on. How long has this been going on exactly, and has it happened before?"

"No sir, Dr. Moore. Now I'm sure there are other things I haven't brought to your attention, but nothing like this has ever concerned me." Cully hesitated as he spoke. "I just don't know what is going on. It's probably nothing, but I wanted to hear it from the horse's mouth." He looked down at his hands and saw they were shaking a little.

Well, tests were run, blood was taken, more blood was taken . . . Cully went through the whole drill that day. He never liked getting stuck with needles, but considering the way he was feeling, he chose to endure it. Of course Mattie wanted the doctors to run every test possible to see why Cully was having symptoms, and he began to wonder if he would be there all day. After a few hours, Dr. Moore returned and said it would be a couple of weeks before they had all the results, so Cully should go home and try to get some extra rest. So he and Mattie checked out and headed toward the car.

They pulled into the garage, got out of the car, and walked inside. There stood Conner and Gaston, waiting to give their parents the familiar loving welcome. *My children have a way of turning a bad moment into a good one,* thought Cully to himself. He thought about how proud he was of both boys, and of how very special they were to him—especially in this moment of uncertainty.

As usual, Conner was pretending he was a pilot flying passengers all over the world. He said, "Dad, welcome to Flight 828. You are now freez to walk about the cabin." Conner was a spirited dreamer who lived life without shame. He kept life in check for the whole family. Cully laughed as he watched his kind and free-spirited boy "flying" around the room. How could he have ever had such unwarranted concerns about having a son with Down syndrome? Cully tried to guess how many times God had found him on his knees, asking for forgiveness and offering thanksgiving at the same time for the son God had given their family. Cully didn't deserve such a blessing—a child who was a joy and a true gift from God. Where would the world be without Conner?

❖

The two weeks they waited on the results felt like two years—especially for Mattie. Then on Tuesday, May 6, 1980, the phone rang. Mattie hustled over to the family phone to see who might be calling at seven in the morning.

"Hello?"

"Good morning, Mrs. Jones. This is Edna Anne Daly from Dr. Moore's office. He would like you and Mr. Jones to come in tomorrow to see him." Mattie asked if everything was okay, but Mrs. Daly said, "Dr. Moore just wants to go over your husband's results."

Moments later Cully was on the way out the door, but he stopped when he noticed a puzzled look on Mattie's face. "Is something wrong?" he asked.

She stared out the window, lost in thought, her arms crossed over her chest. Eyes glazed over, she looked as if she was in another world—one she preferred not to be in. Cully asked her again, "Mats, baby, is everything okay?" Then she lifted her eyes, glanced back at Cully, and smiled weakly.

"Oh honey, that was just the nurse from Dr. Moore's office. He wants to see us tomorrow at 9:30. Your test results are in."

He walked toward the kitchen window that overlooked their deck and the backyard where the boys played, then put his arms around his wife. He held her tightly without saying a word, and she took a deep breath. Together they watched a red cardinal flitting around the handmade cedar birdfeeder on the corner of the back deck. After a few moments, Cully whispered into her ear, "We're going to be okay."

"I know," she said, her eyes focused on the floor. She blinked back tears as her mind raced a mile a min-ute. She and Cully had been down a similar road before—and they would go down this one together too.

❖

After a night of fitful sleep, Mattie and Cully woke up to a cooler than normal spring morning, a slight wind blowing in from the west. For breakfast, Cully had his usual coffee and donut, and Mattie . . . well, she just wasn't hungry. Her mind was thick with thought, and her stomach roiled with dread. She managed a few sips of orange juice before pouring the rest of her cup down the drain.

Even though they found a parking space close to the door, the walk to Dr. Moore's office felt like miles away. Mattie gripped her husband's hand as they made their way inside and down the hall.

"Hello, Mr. Jones," said a friendly assistant at the front desk. Cully checked in for his appointment and then sat down next to wife in the waiting room. He wasn't as nervous as Mattie seemed to be—just curious about what the doctor might say. He had always been an optimistic person and would be able to handle anything thrown at him . . . right? Mattie continued to grip his hand oh so tightly as she locked her beautiful brown eyes on his—as though they were saying their wedding vows all over again. Their hands gripped together, perspiration began to build, as did the anticipation.

Many thoughts ran through Cully's head, but his eyes locked onto a little boy in the corner of the waiting room. The boy sat on the floor trying to figure out a kid's puzzle that had been left in the play area of the office. He was so content just performing this simple task, without a care in the world about what tomorrow would bring him. Glancing back up at Mattie, one thing was for sure: Cully knew how much his wife loved him and how much he loved her. They had been twenty-four and twenty-three years old when they'd said their wedding vows. How lucky he felt to have her and the two boys, all of them living a happy and nor-mal life. Until Dr. Moore walked in and changed their definition of normal.

❖

Having to deal with adversity was nothing new to the family. While Mattie and Cully were dealing with their own challenges, Mattie's sister, Cassidy, was dealing with adversity of her own. For many years, Cassidy and her husband, Blandry, had struggled in marriage, and things weren't getting any better. Not because they lacked love for each other, but because her husband loved other things—namely, money and alcohol. One thing that was for sure: Uncle Blandry was a well-liked guy by most, especially by Gaston and Conner. Ever since Gaston was a little boy, and now that Conner was in the fold, Uncle Blandry had always invested quality time with them. They would go hunting, fishing, and to ball games, and they loved to crack silly jokes together. In spite of his flaws and misfortunes, Uncle Blandry still made as much time as possible to tell his nephews he loved them. And he endeavored to prove it too.

To his credit, Uncle Blandry had been a father figure for the boys. And unlike Aunt Cassidy, Gaston and Conner seemed to overlook Uncle Blandry's faults and bad choices. They loved him for . . . well, for who he was. Aunt Cassidy had tried, but Uncle Blandry had made it nearly impossible for her.

For the three years after's Cully's diagnosis, he and Mattie spent much of their time traveling to Houston for chemo treatments. The boys, in turn, spent more time with extended family as they platooned back and forth between Mamaw and Papaw Lewis and Aunt Cassidy and Uncle Blandry. Gaston's parents didn't get to come to his Babe Ruth baseball games as much as they or he would have liked, so relatives filled in the gaps and made up for lost time during a difficult one. They all knew the boys just wanted Mom and Dad back—and back healthy!

Uncle Blandry was intentional with the boys and took advantage of his time with them. Always seemingly upbeat, Blandry really took to his nephews. They related to each other remarkably. For the past twenty-three years, Blandry had been very successful in the commercial construction business, and his much-respected company, Blanco Inc., built some of the biggest sports arenas in the country. Wealth was something he had a lot of—yet he was not sure if he had much of anything else that counted.

In fact, wealth might even have had Blandry. He bought the boys gifts at every turn—as much as was allowed by Cully and Mattie. A toy, a twenty-dollar bill, a ball, a bike, or anything else they wanted ... He was so generous to the boys and loved them as his own, in spite of being held captive by his past mistakes. As he trudged down a dusty emotional road entangled in heavy chains, he may have loved the boys a little extra to try and make up for what he had lost. Blandry's two were now grown and out of the house—his son, Johnny, and his younger daughter, Karen—and for the most part were out of his life. His relationship with them had been strained for some time over some poor choices he had made early on in his life. The situation was sad for both sides, and the relationship was painful, to say the least. Basically nonexistent.

Gaston and Conner, of course, loved him unconditionally—and not just because of the gifts he gave them (though that sure didn't hurt anything). A private man, Uncle Blandry had never discussed his depression. Fighting inner demons, he was also very generous to Wild Ed's Package Store. He was still battling alcohol abuse, along with health concerns that were due in part to the lifestyle he had chosen to live for many years. Nobody seemed to know but a few members of his immediate family. Gaston, a very intelligent and observant boy, had noticed that Blandry's choices were neither good nor healthy.

In spite of his uncle's shortcomings, Gaston and Uncle Blandry had remained very close over the years, and after Conner arrived on the scene, the three became inseparable. As much as Uncle Blandry loved them, the boys' love was just as strong. Uncle Blandry often got tickled at the "choice words" that his six-year-old nephew was known for. The brutally honest Conner always kept it real without a filter. He lived by Grandmother Lewis's philosophy: "The truth hurts but doesn't kill." He was always the one to tell you when your fly was down or something was hanging out of your nose. But sometimes his wisdom and blunt truth was much harder to hear.

❖

One carefree day, Conner and Gaston were doing what kids do—running around their uncle's workshop, playing around the barn, and enjoying a good game of hide-and-seek. For both of them, the fun part was being found.

Without notice or hesitation, young Conner—spontaneous, straightforward, and intelligent—walked up and found Uncle Blandry in the shop as he piddled with some blueprints for a new stadium in Baltimore that he was getting ready to construct for the professional football team. With that look on Conner's face, Uncle Blandry knew something short and concise was about to be said, whether appropriate or not. Even so, he never could have expected what Conner had to say today.

"Uncle Brandree, you know . . . You know that yous should be going to church. You need to be going so God can heal your problems. You been running with the devil for . . . for . . . far too long. A very long time, it seems. He don't get tired running with you, as long as you let him, of course. You knows your mistakes aren't too big for God. Theys not too big, Uncle Brandree. He's bigger than *all* problems—mines and yours. The devil don't even love you. He just pretends. If you went to church, maybe then you would stop talking to Aunt Cassidy so loud . . . too loud sometimes. She loves you! Like me and Beegee. If you don't get right with her and Jesus, you going to regret it. Your clock don't tick forever, you know. Me and Beegee . . . you know we are here for you always!"

Emotion filled Conner's eyes as he spoke. After pausing to catch his thoughts and his breath, he said, "You know none of us here have forever to get teez things right. The Bible tells me that. Have you read it?"

As if he had been kicked in the gut, Uncle Blandry bent over as he squatted down to his knees. He reached out to hug Conner with a heavy heart, his eyes watering as if he had sliced open a fresh Vidalia onion. No words needed to be said, nor could he even speak in this moment. After a while, he released Conner from the tight hug and turned to look him in the eye. All Uncle Blandry could muster up was, "I know, Conner. You are right. Thank you . . . I love you and I will do better, and—"

"And you never spend time with Johnny and Karen. At least, they don't come see you. I never seez them here. Why is dat? They love you too. And you still got time. Matter of fact, that is all you got right now!" Then Conner turned and ran off to join up with Gaston as if he had never broken stride.

Stunned by what he had just heard, Blandry dropped his head and felt his pride leave him. He walked out of the shop for a few seconds, or maybe a few minutes . . . He was too disoriented to say. The burden of his problems had already been heavy enough on him for many years, but to now have a child reveal wisdom from a genuine, honest perspective was beyond belief. The little man he dearly loved had delivered a cold reality on a rather warm day, using the only kinds of words he knew how to use—true ones.

After walking across the back lawn and in through the back door, Blandry headed straight for his bedroom and fell across his unmade king-size bed, where he wept like never before. How could he be so lost that his young, amazing, and loving nephew could see right through Blandry's cover-up? Outside of his close family, no one else had been able to see him so clearly. He cried out, "Why did I allow this to happen? I have let so many people down. My family, especially my two beautiful kids, and my sacrificing, loving wife . . . They don't deserve any of this." He realized he had been holding on to things that would fade—most very quickly. "Why, God? Help me, Lord! I can't keep living like this. I can't!"

❖

Finally, Mattie and Cully were able to come back home for good. Cully's cancer had gone into remission, or as the doctors said, NED—no evidence of disease. What a happy time that was for all . . . at least for a brief moment.

❖

The sand ran out for Blandry.

Within months of turning fifty-two, and after a flicker of the eyes and a few deep breaths, Uncle Blandry was gone! Conner and Gaston's favorite uncle died of a massive heart attack. This hit the boys hard. Innocent little Conner and big brother Gaston sat saddened yet bewildered at Stevens Memorial Funeral Home as Reverend Paul Shipley gave the eulogy for Mr. Larry Blandry Thomas. He said:

"Today we celebrate the life of Mr. Larry Blandry Thomas. He was born in Hernando, Mississippi, on

August 9, 1931, and he passed on June 7, 1983. Mr. Thomas is survived by his wife, Cassidy Lewis Thomas; his son, Johnny Thomas; and his daughter, Karen Thomas Rivers. Mr. Thomas was a dedicated father and husband. He loved his church, God, and was very involved at Bethel United Methodist. He lived his life the right way and made sure God and family came first. Hard work was a priority. He understood the correct order of things. Today we must celebrate as a Blandry has now entered the gates of heaven and is singing with the angels..."

As Conner sat there, he was very confused—in disbelief at what his ears were hearing. He sometimes missed some things, yet he was confident he'd heard right. That man of the cloth couldn't be serious. Did any of the reverend's words really describe his flailing uncle? Gaston had similar thoughts of his own.

Of course Gaston and Conner were good boys and believers, but believing this about their uncle was something else. It was a tragedy that most people there never knew, never understood what they understood—about the true nature of Blandry's life and the problems he carried to the grave.

Later that day, after Conner and Gaston got back to the house, they both walked directly to the room they shared together and plopped down on their twin beds, each grabbing a pillow in their arms. Neither made a peep, with the exception of some sniffles and heavy breaths—only staring up at the ceiling wondering what it was they had just heard. Not a word was spoken for several minutes until finally

Conner—who was rarely very talkative unless he really had something to say—broke the silence.

"Beegee?" Conner said softly.

"Yes?" Gaston whispered.

"Did you hear what that man, that pastor man said, Beegee?"

"Yes, I heard most of it, or least more than half. Why do you ask?"

"Well, Beegee, um . . . I am not sure I am saying dis right, but . . . Uncle Brandree was so special to both of us. You know, right? And we loved him more than most. And we know he loved us, right? But I have to say something. Dat man didn't . . . Dat pastor man didn't say things the way we knows them to be true. Which makes me wonder if he or others really knew him. I mean, Uncle Brandree point-blank told us one time, when we were squirrel hunting down at the farmland, dat he didn't go to church. He said he didn't know Jesus the way he probably should, but maybe one day when he had time and got everything fixed right dat he would look into it. But he never *did* look into nothing yet, and we knows that. He was a good man, but good man don't gets to heaven on just that alone. My bible say dat.

"He also didn't have many friends, even though he was a friendly man. What dat pastor man said was definitely not what we know as the truth. He didn't know the truth! He was talking bout someone else. What do they call it when people talk about you at a funeral . . . a hulogy? I mean, a eulogy, I think? That was a clown's eulogy, Beegee."

"What's a clown's eulogy, Conner? What do you mean?" said Gaston.

"When people get up and say things at a funeral dat aren't true. Or they think they know somefin or somebody, buts they really don't. You know when people live a certain way, pretending, like a cover-up . . . like they gots it all's together trying to fool certain people or everybody, including themselves. And then . . ." Conner paused. "And then, dat pastor man talking like everybody's going to heaven. It's not right . . . just not." He started to choke up, then tears began making their way down the sides of his cheeks. Even at such a young age, Conner was always one to wear his heart on his sleeve.

He slowly stood from his bed and quietly walked out of the room with his head down and shoulders slumped. Gaston stayed put in silence as his brother walked away. From that moment forward, nothing else was ever said about Blandry's funeral.

EIGHT

*To the world you may be one person, but to one person
you may be the world.*
—*Unknown*

Mattie told Conner about Down syndrome when he was eight years old. She knew he deserved an explanation, but she didn't want it to be the only thing that defined him either. Even so, she spent much of his young life worried that people might not like him because of his difference.

One afternoon she looked at her son and asked him, "So, what do people with Down syndrome look like, Conner?" She did her best to check in with him, to make sure he was okay with who he was.

"Somebody at school says we all looks alike. Is dat right, Mama?"

"Well, Conner, some people may view others in a particular way. Doesn't make it right though. God created us all different, purposeful, and important. Do you ever feel different?" Mattie asked.

Conner—being Conner—was honest. "Sometimes I do. Not all the time. Dere's all kinds of different. Different is tough sometimes, but I am all right. Sometimes I wish theys could just wear my shoes for a day."

Basically, Conner just wanted a fair shake—to be known before he was judged! He could tell when people looked at him strangely, even if he didn't have the right words to explain it. But he tried not to be bothered. He tried to see life as it was, not as others or the world wanted him to see it. One thing was for sure: If you knew him at all, you *really* knew him. But more importantly, he knew you! Facing many challenges early in life might've broken other people, but Conner tried to not let things upset him and focused instead on the good things in every day.

Whenever people asked him what Down syndrome was, he would tell them, "I has an extra chromosome. A doctor will tell yous the extra chromosome causes intellectual disability, which makes it harder for me to learn." Even though some people felt sorry for him, Conner always knew that he could do basically anything anybody else could. Comfortable in his own skin, he didn't need to toot his own horn. He understood that having Down syndrome was part of what made him special. He was grateful and proud of all God had blessed him with.

As he got a bit older, he would also say to the curious folks, "I talk a little different sometimes, but I just want my voice to be heard and appreciated like yous do. My life is similar to yours, if you really thinks about it. I am in the choir at church, on the swim deam . . . I wrote a song with the guitar, play basketball and soccer, ride bikes about as fast as you . . . I watch TV, go fishing and catching the big fish, and do all you does for, the most parts. I try to be a good person and a hard worker. We wants the same things: to be valued and respected. I'm proud of who I am ... I'm like yous!"

❖

As the years gained speed, Conner grew very fond of reading books and listening to inspirational music, even though Gaston had borrowed a few tapes without asking. Conner always joked that his brother "probably needed them more." From what Conner learned every day, he made notes in a journal that continued to give him tips for the future. Once Gaston was grown and had left the house, Conner tried his hardest to be a "normal teenager"—if such a thing exists—and built momentum with the wisdom he had so systematically collected. Before long he had impacted so many lives by sowing the simplest seeds. He was always honest with others, but more importantly, with himself!

Gaston was by far his greatest pride and joy in life. He easily got lost in their enjoyable and quality moments together, even though Gaston—often "too busy" for his little brother—forfeited many of the moments that could've become pleasant memories for the two of them. But no matter. He truly cared unconditionally about people from the get-go, especially his friends and his family—and *especially* Gaston, his hero.

Conner looked for excuses to give a hug (or two) and a strong dose of encouragement, and he wasn't shy to give a touch of his thoughts if needed. If ignorant people made ignorant comments, he exercised patience and kindness anyway. Always encouraging others and giving them something to smile about, Conner lived to make a difference. He rode a wave of enthusiasm and determination, investing in hope and delivering a ripple effect of kindness and compassion to everyone. He also wanted them to understand that they mattered and could do something great with their own lives—if they so chose.

❖

After coming home from a church mission trip to poverty-stricken Haiti with his friends and family at the age of fourteen, Conner had been moved so greatly by the country's damaged foundations that he decided to build one of his own. He sat anxiously in the family room, tapping his foot, waiting impatiently to say something about what he'd learned. He had called a family meeting, planning to discuss the idea he'd had and how to turn it into action.

Once his parents joined him, Conner—with fire in his belly—said, "Well, it's about time yous got here! And it's about time I do something. To start something new takes effort, but we needs to move. Nothing can stop me from trying and doing. When people hurt, I hurt too. Now it's time for me to help them . . . and I will. I want to give the world a peek of what I learned in Haiti—that everyone matters. Everyone really matters."

❖

Conner's project began with selling some items he had made at the afternoon community class he attended. He wanted to raise money for deaf children and assistance programs that helped them navigate the world. He then created a coat and shoe donation-drop service called Warm Feet at certain locations around the city of Hernando, and eventually Memphis too. But Conner's good works did not end there.

Before long, and with help from Cully and Mattie, Conner had established 47 Matters: an umbrella organization designed to provide shoes and warmth to the homeless, and to pay for skill-training programs for disabled persons. By then, a lot of kids his age were driving cars—yet he was driven to do something more amazing. Life was everything to Conner!

Conner paid it forward over the years. The momentum built, and 47 Matters eventually spread to Boston, Philadelphia, and Chicago—Conner's cities of choice. By the time Conner was in his early twenties, the foundation had enough steam to launch a national television marketing campaign. They acquired some heavy-hitting partners and donors, and acquired sponsors on five major sports networks. There was no stopping Conner from trying and doing—just as he'd said that day on his parents' couch. He was going to change the world, one life at a time.

NINE

*The greatest obstacle to achieving my goals is that
I don't know what my goals are.*
—Ashleigh Brilliant

When William Ben Jones had retired from the oil business with the Amoco Corporation, the family had moved to the mid-South just east along the Mississippi River, on the fourth Chickasaw Bluff near Memphis, Tennessee, to be closer to family and a fresh start. They had settled in the small northern Mississippi border community area of DeSoto County, where Cully Jones would finish high school with an honorable three-sport athletic career. Years later, Gaston would follow suit through the Hernando school system, hoping to eventually walk in the footsteps of his father and grandfather, who had found success and happiness through their work.

Many years rolled by, and Gaston graduated from high school and Rhodes College across from Overton Park and the Memphis Zoo. He did well there, excelling while taking several elective acting classes at the prestigious Midtown school. Perhaps his gift for improv and the stage hinted at the role he was preparing the play.

Gaston's debut role was charging ahead into the real world—the place he had always heard and read about. He wasn't exactly "off to join the circus," but he was ready to pursue his lifelong dream of being part of "The Greatest Show on Earth." He was hoping for world renown, but for what, he wasn't quite sure. With no clear plan or direction, and unsure of where he was headed or what he wanted to become, he settled for some vague notion of success. One thing was for sure: He would perform at a high level and have success at whatever he did.

With six figures in his sights, Gaston was prepared to set sail for a very happy and elite financial future. Yet little did he know that his bags were packed for an unforeseeable, rock-bottom destination.

❖

Gaston's father, his grandfather, and their fathers had generally worked at one job or with one company all their lives before retiring—but Gaston's path diverged. By age thirty-one he was chasing "the American Dream"—climbing the corporate brown-nosing ladder, winning awards, and trying to fill the big shoes of a wealthy uncle. At moments it was more about keeping up with the Joneses than anything else, which in time grew increasingly frustrating. Being the national director of sales and running a business was what he'd been hired to do, but as it turned out, everybody and everything seemed to be running him. The higher he jumped and the faster he ran, the more he ended up on his backside or in a backslide, wondering if he could get up to do it again... and again... and again.

Gaston knew life could at times be dark, but he had let himself go to a deep, deep place. In his heart he knew some serious questions needed to be asked... and more importantly, answered. Feeling as if he was on a runaway rail car, he couldn't even get past the basic questions of life. He wondered, *Who am I? Does anyone else wonder or think the same?* These questions lingered in his mind whenever a free moment existed. Maybe the real question was *whose* was he becoming? He hoped against hope that life would slow down long enough for him to jump off the hamster wheel and figure out how to change course. Even his truth was a lie—a side effect of living an unexamined and purposeless life.

Before long, Gaston's existence was a full three-ring production. His first job turned into his second, which turned into his third, fourth, fifth, and beyond. As the world screamed for his attention, trying to name him and tell him who he should be, he wondered if he would die before he discovered the real reason he was born. From city to city, his performance garnered more fans and grew in sophistication. To outsiders, he was selling tickets to the Gaston Show hand over fist—but in reality, the only thing he was selling was *out!*

Thirty-five years into to this thing they call life, and Gaston was single, lonely, and miserable. Time had somehow escaped rapidly over the years. He was so far away from his true self that at times he wondered if God recognized him or knew where he was. The questions came quickly with no answers. Maybe the questions weren't good ones. This was not what Gaston thought he had signed up for in this thing they called "The Real World."

❖

Gaston's Magnanni "Carlito" Cap Toe Derby shoes hit the hardwoods as he walked from the garage into the house—his dark hiding place of four walls. He had just come home from a long and intense West Coast trip from San Diego after a brief stopover in Denver, and guilt nagged at him as he glanced down at his phone and saw five missed calls from Conner. Feeling sorry and frustrated, among other things, he dropped his bags on the floor and crashed on the couch in front of the fifty-inch big screen.

He was just plain exhausted and empty from trying to find happiness. He had dated several girls and had been in relationships, but for whatever reason, they just hadn't worked out. Nice cars? Check. Nice houses? Check. Nice, extravagant trips? Check. Money? Check. According to some standards, he should have been married already with at least two beautiful kids, a dog, a cat, and a white picket fence. That was just how it was supposed to play out based upon all the movies and fairy tales ... right?

Growing up in little ol' DeSoto County, Gaston had envisioned that sort of future for himself. But still with no answers or family of his own, the only way he knew to combat this void was by always running faster, jumping higher, pleasing whomever he needed to please. A life of distraction, deception, and busyness was all he knew. He had learned the act: how to be whoever he needed to be to get by.

Gaston had not yet learned that he was giving away his life for nothing! Work obligations had set him in such a tailspin that he often lost track of which way was up. And as for those answers he hoped for? Well, when he was honest with himself, he knew he wasn't really looking that hard—at the very least, he was looking in the wrong places. He had never sought out people of wisdom and perspective, running instead in the same circles of people who were most likely lost themselves. No matter the people who moved in and out of his life, it was still just a circus for Gaston; performing as different characters, they told him what he wanted to hear, applauded his success, and presented him daily with a bag of fool's gold—while he did the same for them. It was the same routine, over and over, no matter where Gaston landed for work. The next day he would pack his bags, board a plane, and pre-pare himself for the next show

❖

As Gaston lay on his couch, weary and blurry-eyed, he pondered his unraveling reality. What a "Bozo" he had become! He had always heard that "Luck favors the prepared"—but he had done nothing to succeed for a life of true happiness. Instead, he felt miserably "lucky." A younger colleague had asked him a few years back, "Gaston, who is behind all your great accomplishments? You know they always say there is someone helping you." He thought to himself, *Do you mean "Who's behind the mask I am wearing?"*

He was a wreck and a bad one. The pieces had shattered everywhere, and he wondered if the pieces could ever be put back together again. As if she were standing right in front of him, he heard the words from his late grandmother, Mamaw Lewis: "Gaston, no matter how broken you feel, God can and will make a beautiful mosaic out of all the broken pieces . . . if you are willing to let Him. If you are still here, it is because *He is not finished with you.* So get up and live with intention. Be what you were created for. A rearview mirror is for seeing what is behind you—not for seeing what's ahead. Choose to go in a new direction. And choose well!"

TEN

The greatest tragedy is not death, but a wasted life.
—Unknown

Gaston watched the deer walking curiously along his ten acres, munching on grass and some clover with her spotted baby fawn by her side. He sat, pencil in hand, rocking the front porch swing slightly, as the morning dew burned off his picturesque front lawn. Trying for a change to live in the moment, he could only ponder and reflect as he flipped through some of the coffee-stained pages of a long, winding journal he had scribbled in over time. Almost too painful at times to swallow, he poured over the blue lines of thoughts he'd once recorded.

Time is bleeding out at an astonishing rate, as if my life is hemorrhaging away. The years just seem to be screaming by . . .

He understood his margin for error was shrinking. From twenty-five to twenty-nine, from thirty-one to thirty-four . . . and now at the ripe old age of forty-one, he had no doubt that his life was a complete mess. He glanced at his phone and the list of missed calls . . . voicemail after voicemail from Conner, conversation after conversation he'd been too busy to have. He wondered how long it had been since they'd last talked.

He thought about his bighearted and unconditionally loving little brother. Perhaps the saddest part of Gaston's decline was that Conner still believed his brother had hung the moon. Conner couldn't have been more proud of Gaston and thought he was the happiest and highest achieving person he had ever known. Gaston had jumped over and through many hoops through the years, but clearing the moon was just one of numerous feats he hadn't accomplished. For some reason unknown to Gaston, Conner had wanted to grow up and be like his brother.

Predictably, every time Conner saw his brother, he told Gaston how amazing his life was. He thought Gaston had everything in life that a person could ever want. To him, Gaston was the true definition of success . . . yet the tragedy of it all was that Gaston's life had little significance. Conner's assessment couldn't have been further from the truth—which was why Gaston had been avoiding his calls of late. Was he misleading his little brother, who battled an unfair health challenge every single day of his life? Without fully understanding why, Conner also battled unwarranted ridicule and judgment from strangers who, for the most part, were empty-spirited like Gaston. Even though Conner rose above it, it was unfortunate that he could never avoid the stigma of unfair and ignorant opinions. It broke Gaston's heart to know that he had no excuses for the bad lifestyle choices he had made, whereas Conner had a much harder life out of no fault of his own.

Forty-four candles in, Gaston needed a reality check—but he did not expect the test awaiting him. One early September morning, while eating breakfast with his mom at Merridee's Coffee and Breakfast in Hernando, he learned that his dad's cancer had returned. Cully was not doing as well as everyone had hoped, and his new prognosis was poor. The cancer had spread beyond cure.

Gaston didn't know what to say or do. Trying to process what Conner, Mattie, and Gaston were about to experience felt impossible. Not to mention Cully . . . How must he be feeling, facing what he did? Life was happening—again! That afternoon, Mattie, Conner and Gaston piled into the car and headed to Baptist Memorial Hospital–DeSoto, just about ten minutes down the road in Southaven. The only sound in the car was silence.

Struggling to put one in front of the other, Gaston walked into the hospital and down a long, white hallway to the elevator near the cafeteria. Everything moved in slow motion, except for the "why" that chased his reasoning. Conner pushed the button to the second floor, and up they went.

Cully lay covered in white sheets, in a room across the hall from the nurses' station. Many tubes were hooked to his body due to some internal and external bleeding, and to Gaston, he looked sicker than ever before. He had lost his hair to chemo and had grown thinner and thinner, but he was as happy and grateful to see his family as they were to see him.

After visiting for some time, Gaston tenderly wrapped his arms around his dad's frail body. Looking deep into his bright blue but weary eyes, Gaston told him how much he loved him, then kissed him on his cool forehead. Gaston could barely catch his breath. Cully gripped his hand and brushing his son's face gently, mustering up enough energy to tell Gaston how much he loved him in return. Tired, he took two deep breaths, paused, and peacefully shared a few soft-spoken words: "I'm so proud of you, son, but I'm ready to go home. He is calling me there. You must carry the torch and protect our family's respected name."

Gaston had never felt so fragile. As he held his father as tightly as possible, the only thing he could let go of was the emotion that poured out. Then he hugged Conner and his mother and told them how much they meant to him, how much he loved them, and how blessed his life had been to have them in it. Staying true, they linked hands as their weak, yet strong, earthly father prayed. Finishing their goodbyes, Conner and Gaston walked out into the hallway as their mother closed the door for some time. From the outside, they heard the sounds of heartbreak.

❖

Life changed in an instant. Little did Gaston know that this visit would be the last time he would see his dad on this broken earth. The Father had already called Cully home, and as Gaston sought explanations, he felt that life as he'd known it was no longer . . . well, as he had known it. Thick in thought and heavy in heart, he lashed out at God. *God, why are You doing this?* This wasn't what life was supposed to be, was it? How could a person live with sadness of this kind?

Gaston thought he had signed up for the happy life early on. Uncle Blandry was gone, and now Dad. If God knew everything, why couldn't He explain this one to Gaston? As hard as this moment was, as his mother and Pastor Jim had reiterated, Gaston knew the "Good Book" spoke of a hope and a future—and Gaston trusted it! His dad had left a legacy—one Gaston longed to carry on.

❖

Hours after burying Cully, Gaston, Conner, and Mattie returned to the home place they'd known for more than forty years. As Gaston walked down the house's stained aggregate driveway, his eyes locked on his old basketball goal and its tethered net. A worn, synthetic Spaulding basketball, given to him and Conner dozens of years back, lay off to the side in the yard. The memories were fresh for Gaston—just how often over the years that little orange ball had become therapy for him in more ways than most could possibly ever understand. He picked up the neglected ball and gave it a few dribbles, surprised that it had maintained some bounce. As he moved around his familiar court, he thought about being newly hard-pressed with real-life questions and new responsibilities. Glancing up at the goal that once held his future, he couldn't help but wonder how much time remained on his game clock.

He took a shot, but the ball bounced off the rim. For some time he had missed the mark on life, and now he missed his encourager, his ball thrower, his tackler . . . the proud father who'd always made time to tell his son that he loved him. As Gaston stood, tossing the ball from one hand to the other, he reflected on the moments with his dad. *How I have taken them for granted!* he thought. Cully had always told him to live as if every day was his last. And to his credit, that is how his dad had lived.

ELEVEN

Honesty is the first chapter of the book of wisdom.
—Thomas Jefferson

A few weeks after his father passed, Gaston left his house and drove downtown to the local shoe parlor to get some shine and repair—but not for his shoes.

Thanks to Cully's influence, Gaston was still a regular at the Evans's Shoe Shine Parlor all these years later. Gaston had been grandfathered in. He understood how much the parlor had meant to the community of Hernando; and he couldn't have adequately explained how valuable the parlor had been to him personally. The senior George Evans, now getting up there in years, had recently passed the reins over to his son Maurice. A chip off the old block, Maurice picked up right where his father had left off, and the normal way of things hadn't missed a beat. Maurice had a different tone, but the same voice as his father.

Having stood shoulder to shoulder with Gaston's whole family at Cully's funeral just a month or so prior, the Evanses had supported Gaston inside the parlor and out. Matter of fact, Mr. George had stood up and said a few heartfelt words during the memorial service that had stirred Gaston to tears. The connection between the Evanses and the Joneses was blind to color and felt more like blood than mere friendship. Mr. George's heart ran rampant with love and serving in a truly remarkable way.

As Gaston walked into the parlor with a pair of worn boots in hand, his heart was the heaviest thing he carried. It was a rather unique occasion because both the senior George and Mr. Maurice were there at the same time and had seen Gaston pulling into one of the few vacant parking spaces right in front of the store's marquee. As Gaston reached for the well-scuffed brass nickel knob, the door opened ahead of him and he saw two black men standing side-by-side and looking at him with welcoming smiles on their faces. Even more, he recognized the care and compassion in their eyes as something he had seen many times before.

With arms outstretched, George and Maurice grabbed Gaston and hugged him tight. There was no "hello" or "how are you" because words weren't necessary. After what felt like five minutes of being squeezed by an anaconda, Gaston was turned loose. Both men looked him in the eye before saying almost simultaneously, "We love you, Mr. Gaston Jones."

"God has received an angel," said Mr. George. "Of course He just loaned your father out to us. We know that. You know that. Mr. Jones touched many lives and will continue to inspire a legacy of gratitude and serving." He paused to clear his throat. "And he gave so much, you always thought he was giving to everybody except himself. We now must shine on until we receive our call to come home and join Him. To ask why is normal, but not best. We know this moment is a tough one, but we will help you take care of Mrs. Mattie and Mr. Conner. It's our privilege and our pledge! They are ours, as are you. Now, come on now and let's get those boots cleaned up. God knows you and I are still here for an awesome purpose. People are waiting on you out there to do what only you can."

Mr. George gave Gaston a hearty pat on the shoulder, then turned and walked toward the back and disappeared the way he had for many years. Gaston, trying to hold back a tear or two, chuckled to himself that Mr. George could so easily walk away from such an impassioned speech. One thing was for sure: Gaston knew George and Maurice had his back. That was understood.

As Gaston settled into his chair, Mr. Maurice chose to put a polish and shine not only on Gaston's boots, but also on his spirit and direction. "Mr. Jones, shoot straight with me. How are you holding up?"

"I am good, Mr. Maurice," Gaston said, out of convenience more than anything. "It sure is a beautiful day today."

Pausing for a moment, Mr. Maurice lifted his head up and stared out the window as a car or two passed. He collected his words before turning to face his customer again. Looking Gaston in the eyes, he said, "Mr. Jones, hear me now. It is *always* a great day. Even though some days feel better than others, if you choose to look through the eyes of those with greater troubles than your own, you will gain a sense of gratitude like no other."

Gaston didn't quite know what to say, so he nodded and let Maurice continue.

"I suppose people are a lot like the shoes I shine," Maurice said. "They are worn, cut up, marked deeply . . . yet when properly cared for, they can look sharp every time you see them. They come in many colors, shapes, and sizes, and many have traveled a tough mile or two—yet they keep walking and eventually become even better when broken in. Some cost less and some cost more, yet all are of equal value to the man above. That includes you, Mr. Jones!"

"Maurice, let's say I want to be a better man and live a better life—but I don't know if I have anything to offer anyone. What advice would you give me?"

Maurice chuckled as he carried on with his work. "Some days, a smile and a word of hope is all that we can give people—yet the *choice* to influence and to try to make a difference even during our own challenging times is the key. Encouragement goes a long way for people. You got it, Mr. Jones?"

Gaston nodded, though he inwardly continued to question his ability to influence anyone for the better. In his heart he knew he had missed so many opportunities to put his best foot forward for his own friends and family—let alone for the troubled and hurting. How could he make time for people when he spun his rat-race wheel almost every waking hour of his life?

"Sometimes I think I've lost my way, Maurice. I hear your wise words but don't know when or how to put them into action. Every day is so busy that I can barely make time to call my own brother on the phone... What am I doing wrong?"

"I'm keepin' it real here, Mr. Jones. Let's be honest. You always seem to be searchin' for that next big thing. Do you think you will ever find it? That next big thing ain't lost. You is."

Maurice put his head down and went back to work with a deep brown base coat of Kiwi polish. As Gaston remained quiet, he considered how his friend's perspective on life—freely given—was actually worth a pot of gold. He hoped those wise words could soak into a hardened and hurting heart.

"Yes, sir," responded an embarrassed, yet dejected, Gaston. Maurice couldn't have been more spot-on.

❖

As Gaston pulled his car out of the shoe shine parlor's parking lot, he was almost breathless. Maurice's words had humbled him, for sure, and he had suddenly become grateful that no one else remained in the shop to observe what could've easily turned into a breakdown. Yet one question plagued him as he made his way through Hernando: *Does everyone see through me this easily?* He thought he had done such a great job of camouflaging his pain, hiding his failures and frustrations without a hint of covered tracks. In that moment Gaston felt seen, but had he really been seen by intuitive friends and acquaintances who had played along with his game of make-believe? *Surely Maurice is exceptional,* he thought to himself. *No one else has seen me this clearly.*

What a waste his life had become. Life had given him so many opportunities, so many chances, and he had squandered them all. He couldn't live this way—let alone die this way. All he seemed to have to his name in that moment was a whole lot of nothing.

❖

Days later, as he sat at his desk at work, Gaston looked up and saw his boss approaching. He'd never cared for the man and couldn't imagine that opinion changing. "Gaston, can we meet tomorrow morning for a few minutes in my office?"

Well, great, Gaston thought to himself. *Might as well dump some more news on my head since I have everything else figured out.*

He didn't know what this would be about, yet it couldn't be too good, right? Nothing else was good in his life at the moment. "Sure, Jack. What time tomorrow?"

"How about nine thirty? That will give you time to make some calls and do whatever you need to do beforehand."

Gaston did his best to appear agreeable, though he hadn't planned on coming into the office until later that morning. "Yes, that will be perfect," he said. "See you then."

After Jack sauntered away, Gaston stood from his desk and headed to the restroom. He opened the door and glanced in the mirror once or twice, frustrated by worry. Why on earth did his VP want to meet with him tomorrow? He rubbed his temples at the headache that threatened and ran through a mental list of what this could possibly mean. As he looked at his own face in the mirror and tried to recognize the man he saw, he wondered if getting fired would be the greatest relief of his adult life.

❖

The next morning, he walked into Jack's office at the appointed time. Overnight Gaston's imagination had run wild with possibilities for what Jack might want to talk about, but what eventually happened he never could've predicted.

"So, Gaston," said Jack, settling back into his leather chair, "I need you to represent us at a charity auction that's coming up for one of the nonprofits we sponsor." He snorted. "You know, one of those groups we sponsor for the write-offs."

Gaston let out the breath he'd been holding. "Why, sure, Jack. I don't see why not."

"You'll need to make some remarks, some hogwash comments about how we're so proud of the work we're doing together, blah blah blah ... I figured you'd be best for the job since it's one of those pathetic mongoloid charities." He looked down and began moving papers around on his desk.

Gaston had heard that word more times than most, and he'd hoped to never hear it again. As he looked for the right way to tell his boss as much, the words got stuck in his throat.

"You can go now, Gaston. I'll have Sherry get you details about the auction." Jack waved him out without even making eye contact.

As Gaston stood to leave, he seethed with anger. He wanted to pound his fist on the desk and sling the stack of sales results he held in his hand across the floor. But instead, he just silently escaped the room and let his heart drop into his stomach.

He spent the next hour fighting the urge to go back and set his boss straight. This wasn't the first occasion Jack had used such language or made similar comments about people like Conner, but Gaston had let it go every time. *He's picked a fight with the wrong guy,* Gaston told himself. *This time he's going to learn a lesson.*

But Gaston remained glued to his chair, trying to muster up the courage to defend his brother. Eventually he grabbed his computer and headed to the parking lot, overwhelmed by guilt and fury. He was headed to the West Coast for several days, so he figured he could justify working from home instead. He threw his belongings onto the passenger seat and slammed the driver's side door, then took a few deep breaths before starting the engine.

As Gaston pulled onto Northside Drive, the phone rang. He looked down at the caller ID and saw the name of the one who actually had it all together—the all-American guy who was the epitome of happiness. Shame pinged in Gaston's gut. If Conner only knew how amazing he was and how broken his brother had become. "Hello, my superstar. How is your day going, buddy? How is my favorite brother doing?"

"Beegee, I sure do miss you and love you. When will I see you next? Will I see you soon? Are you coming home today?"

Gaston's heart churned inside his chest. How could someone love him so much in spite of his pathetic circus act? Faking it for what had become practically a lifetime? "Brother, I sure have been missing you too."

"Beegee, you know I am proud of you, right? You're gonna be the president one day." A half laugh was all Gaston could muster. Feeling dejected and worthless, Gaston tried to swallow the lump in his throat at the thought of how he'd failed his brother only moments before.

As Gaston drove and talked to his brother, the sun dropped below the tree line—yet darkness had set in his life long before. He had a place to live, but nowhere felt like home anymore. The enemy had set up camp right in his backyard and obscured the windows that otherwise would've let in the light. At the end of every day he laid his empty and miserable head onto a cold, lonely pillow and closed his eyes on another wasted day. How many of those days remained? Only God Himself could know.

TWELVE

*Time is all you have. And you may find one day
that you have less than you think.*
—Randy Pausch

After two days of meetings in San Diego and another day's worth in Texas, Gaston had checked into room 1124 at the Four Seasons Hotel in downtown Dallas. As he undressed from another day in the rat race, he overheard the voice of Alyssa Darling—the dirty-blonde news reporter on local channel KDFW. He looked over his shoulder as he unbuttoned his white collared shirt, listening to the interview with a man in a curly red wig.

"Being a clown is rewarding, because you can connect with the audience and live a happy, fulfilling, and entertaining life," said the fool in a clown costume.

"And what led you to a life in the circus, Mr. Schultz?"

Gaston rolled his eyes. He walked toward the bed and draped his blue striped tie across the pillow, then hit the Off button on the TV remote. "Gimme a break," he said aloud to himself. At one point in time, he might've believed such a thing about the clown's life—but no longer. Heck, he was a veteran performer at the youthful age of forty-seven. "Ask *me* for the facts, Alyssa! You're talking about an identity crisis, pal!"

Gaston had run himself into the ground. Staring out the hotel window in a daze, he watched the busyness of the freeway off in the distance and wondered if the world would keep on moving at this pace if he were no longer in it. He knew it would.

I'd better stop clowning before it's too late. The big tent I've been performing in could come crashing down at any moment.

Gaston's lifestyle also looked like a circus—zipping back and forth across America for work, searching for what he presumed he wanted. Was this what people called "the American Dream"? He wrestled with the past and present, but there was no greater enemy than the one staring back at him when he looked in the mirror.

Some people grow up knowing they want to become a lawyer. Others know that becoming an elementary school teacher is their calling. But this particular small-town, simple Mississippi boy was still trying to figure it out. He had contemplated his options over the years, but things had to change quickly if he wanted to alter his course. He was running out of time, and by now, he had something else to worry about: his health. Now more often than not, Gaston's head throbbed and his heart raced. As he continued to wind down for the day, he riffled through his toiletry bag for some Tylenol and some immediate relief.

Gaston had some very important meetings the next day in Orlando, and he hoped to organize his things as he prepared his presentations. With such a long day ahead of him, all he wanted was a relaxing night. After a steamy shower, he was moments away from a good night's rest when—*BAM!* He collapsed across the foot of the king bed, the television still blaring in the background.

❖

Gaston never would have awoken were it not for the pounding noise he heard coming from his door.

"Housekeeping!"

What time was it? Had he overslept? What about his flight? Oh no ... He didn't even remember getting into bed ... He looked at the clock and gasped. How could it possibly be ten o'clock already?

"Housekeeping!"

"Just a moment!" he cried. He stood and quickly splashed water on his face, taking in the marks along the side of his face that were signs of a deep, deep sleep. How on earth had this happened?

Over and under, pulling through ... He tied the best hurried knot he could and threw on a sport blazer to make himself look presentable. He scrambled to pack up his bags before apologizing to the housekeeper on his way out. He sped away in a taxi, desperately hoping to get there before his flight departed for MCO. He mopped the sweat from him brow as they weaved in and out of traffic, confused by how he'd managed to sleep so long through his alarm.

To his dismay, several things were going on now

that did not make sense. As they passed the skyscrapers and the busy, congested streets on the way to the airport, he had the gut feeling that something was going to have to give. His life might even depend upon it.

❖

Fifteen minutes before wrapping up a two-hour presentation that afternoon, Gaston began to sway. Embarrassed, he asked for a moment to collect himself before collapsing into a chair. The people around him scurried about, wondering if they should get him some water or call an ambulance, but all Gaston could think about was the shortness of breath and the tightness and discomfort in his chest. Before long he had been lifted onto a gurney, and an ambulance sped toward Florida Hospital Orlando, the nearest ER. He was diagnosed with dehydration, fatigue, and severe stress—the kinds of ailments a man could inflict upon himself. All he wanted to do was go home to Hernando to recover and regroup after the worst health scare he'd ever ex-perienced.

❖

The room couldn't have been any colder as Gaston sat in the doctor's office, waiting, and waiting, and waiting. For many reasons, he didn't feel right about this moment. His insides churned and rolled like the five-story red Ferris wheel at the local county fair on South Industry Parks Boulevard. For quite possibly the first time in his life, he wanted to be completely transparent—and he dreaded the fate he was soon to hear.

"Good morning, Gaston," said Dr. Noostrom as he entered the exam room. "I understand you've suffered a health setback within the last couple of days. Is that correct?"

"Yes, sir," a nervous Gaston responded.

"Not good, to say the least. You know, for years you have been under too much stress. And you've ignored some things that just won't disappear on their own. Of course, putting off changing your habits has not helped the cause," said Dr. Noostrom. "The latest episode in Orlando does not surprise me. You also know your family history and how important it is to take care of yourself. Right?"

Gaston nodded. Noostrom had known him for years, so he trusted the man's judgment and opinion.

The physician glanced up from his notes and took a hard look at his patient. "Honestly, you just don't seem like yourself for some reason, Gaston. You're putting on a good front, but I just sense something is off." He paused. "You know, most people live for the approval of others. They spend all their time thinking about what others think of them instead of doing what's best for themselves."

"You're right, Doc," Gaston said, noting his doctor's sincerity.

Dr. Noostrom reviewed the results of the various tests Gaston had endured at the hospital. He reminded Gaston that cholesterol doesn't manage itself, and neither do stress or sugar levels. Gaston sighed and nodded as he took in the information, wondering to himself how he'd ever have the time to make the changes he needed to make.

"One more thing, if I may, Gaston: Do whatever it takes to get your life in order. Be the healthiest version of yourself. Live life fully in every moment. I see far too many with fewer abilities and smarts, but their candle just burns out far too soon. With such an engaging and dynamic personality, you should expect more from yourself. I know Conner thinks the world of you! Life is already too short. You don't need to help it along."

Gaston had not expected such a spiel from his family doctor, whom he'd known since he was much younger. The brutal truth went straight to his heart, and he wondered if Dr. Noostrom and Mr. Maurice had been in contact with each other. Both men had seen right through his once-impervious mask. Was he really fooling anybody anymore?

A few pricks and a "see you in two weeks" later, Gaston was out the door—only briefly stopping by the front desk to grab his next appointment card.

❖

Gaston dreaded the two-week follow-up with Doctor Noos (as he called him). As the nurse stepped out, she said, "The doctor will be in shortly," before dropping Gaston's chart on the back of the closing door. The only thing he could think about was the shadow of darkness that hovered over his unfortunate reality. He had been running all his life in search of a perfect sunset—and now the sunset of his life was upon him. Anxiously awaiting the doctor, he kept thinking about a conversation he'd had as a teenager with his grandmother: "The best place for us to be is where God wants us to be."

Another of her simple nuggets of wisdom. But how could God want Gaston to be here—middle-aged, stuck in a waiting room, unsure of every life choice he'd ever made? It was also pretty apparent that God didn't want Gaston to continue living the life he had chosen up to this point. What a waste! Gaston could only guess how disappointed he would've been to his grandparents, had they been living. Not to mention Conner.

When Dr. Noostrom strode into the room with his nurse, Gaston was not prepared for the news he was about to receive. Surely he had time to make his life right . . . right? By the look on the doctor's face, Gaston knew that this conversation was about to be worse than he'd hoped. He was about to learn what if felt like to be hit with a ten-pound hammer.

"Mr. Jones, your vitals are not so favorable, and the test results do show prostate cancer. The conditions aren't as advantageous as we would like, yet this kind of cancer is treatable and beatable," he said confidently.

"What? What are you talking about?" Gaston couldn't think fast enough to understand what the doctor was saying. The air was just too heavy to breathe.

"You have cancer, Gaston."

Sweat broke out on Gaston's forehead as he struggled to speak. He opened his mouth, but no words came.

"You have some options, and the prognosis is good—yet no one should make promises about results. You'll have a hill to climb. Success will be determined in large part by how committed you are to living a better, healthier life. You'll need to change your priorities a bit and live more intentionally. It will require ... well, basically, changing yourself! The ball is in your court," said Dr. Noostrom.

Gaston still felt paralyzed, as if hit by a high-powered Taser. To Dr. Noostrom and his nurse, Gaston had the look of a Carolina Chickadee that had just flown into a kitchen windowpane. In his mind he heard the sweet little voice of his Mamaw Lewis: "We can do this. We got this. Just turn your life around before it is too late. Commit to what matters, son!"

Gaston didn't believe a person could hear words from heaven, but maybe he had an angel in his corner. Maybe God had put her up to sharing this message while there was still time. Though not sure he believed in that kind of thing, he sure heard it echoing loud and clear.

❖

Driving with a new sense of purpose, Gaston couldn't move fast enough to the solitude in the woods down Mill Hollow Road. Hernando was home, and all he needed was to be there now, sitting on his front porch swing. He hadn't been there since . . . well, for a long while. Through the years—for too many of them, he was starting to see—he had overlooked and taken for granted this peaceful place, where crickets sang of happiness in the tall grass and mockingbirds chirped with joy at the rising sun. In his woods the rabbits hopped to the blessing of the morning dew, and puppies rolled around with the thrill of brotherhood. In Hernando, big problems seemed less big. It truly was a town where everything seemed to move a little slower, and Gaston was in desperate need of a pace adjustment. As he drove, his thoughts turned toward Conner and how much they, as brothers, needed each other. Gaston found himself amid one of life's darkest moments to date, and "the show" couldn't go on any longer. Pulling into his winding driveway, lined with pear orchards galore, he reached down under the passenger seat to grab the wadded-up brochure he had created only months prior. It read: "Home for Sale on Ten Picturesque Acres . . . Come Find Your Dream Home and Enjoy Some Simplicity and Peace of Mind!" *Wow,* he thought to himself. *What a mistake selling this house would have been.* It was time to make changes, to find his purpose, and to start living for it.

❖

Gaston spent the weekend at home, resting a bit and coming to grips with his diagnosis. He called his mother and his brother to break the news, and he was grateful for the time to reflect on what to do with himself in the weeks to come. But soon enough life came calling again, and before the weekend was through, Gaston was already preparing for another long work trip. Just one more before some longer time off the road and before, hopefully, a life reset. Just one more...

Hitting four cities on the first leg of a four-day trip, he had just wrapped up a meeting with important clients in Germantown, Tennessee, as he pulled into the covered long-term parking garage at the Memphis International Airport. With bags packed and laptop in hand, Gaston checked in for his first flight of the week. Oh how he looked forward to relaxing a bit after his return.

Smartphones and headphones were glued to ears all around him. He plopped down amid a row of yellow chairs in Terminal B, waiting for the boarding call at his gate. He was on the way to Orlando before hitting Atlanta and then wrapping up in Raleigh. Tomorrow's main meeting materials rested on his lap, and he anxiously shuffled them around as he thought about how much was at stake with these meetings. At boarding call, he was first on the plane—a perk of having a Gold Card Flight Member status. As he settled in, an at-tractive and seemingly kind flight attendant stopped by to greet him and take his drink order. As she set his drink on the pull-out tray, his Apple iPhone Plus buzzed with an overflow of texts and emails. He took another long sip off the rocks, pondering the familiar old question: *How will all of this end... if ever?*

THIRTEEN

I don't think of all the misery but of all the beauty that remains.
—Anne Frank

Conner looked up toward a canvas of blue. No cloud in the sky marred it. As he and Mattie headed home from his Ability First work program, Conner blurted out, "Look, Mom. We got our shiny brues again"—a phrase he often used on a bright and sunny day when the only thing that could seem to interrupt the blue was a few jet lines zigzagging across the sky.

Mattie chuckled and smiled at her son. Maybe it was a good time for another check-in. "You're so cheerful and kind, Conner. Have you ever met anyone who didn't like you? Have people ever said mean things to you about Down syndrome?"

A resounding "no, ma'am" ran through his head and came calmly out of his mouth. "At least, not the ones who took their time and gots to know me," he mumbled. He usually didn't talk as much as he listened, but when he did speak, you knew something heartfelt or important was coming.

The way he saw it, the only difference between him and others was that he had a little something extra—

that forty-seventh chromosome, to be exact! "Mom, several years ago, right after our trip to Haiti, I drew the line in the sand. I says to myself, *No performing or pretending to get others to like me.*" Conner stared out the car window as they drove down their street and past their next door neighbor's house. He laughed when he saw the neighbor's dog, Biscuit, running across the front yard.

Of course several decades before, at the ripe old age of fourteen, he had pledged to be true to himself and make every day count. After his trip to Haiti, he had been filled with the passion and determination to make a difference—and he had. The 47 Matters foundation was still going strong, and Conner had changed more lives over the years than he'd ever truly understand.

As a boy he had overheard Gaston telling Mom and Dad about his unsung hero, Dr. William Sheads—a philanthropist and world-changer. The man was famous for doing good and awarding others who did the same. Conner had even seen a special on *60 Minutes* one Sunday evening back in his early twenties about The SHEADS Foundation and the prestigious SHEADS Award that Dr. Sheads bestowed on a public servant each year. The award had piqued Conner's interest and driven him to do and be even more. Dr. Sheads's famous statement, "Make it fun or funny. Make a difference. It's a choice!" just stuck in Conner's mind like chewed gum on the bottom of the kitchen table. From that day forward, he did . . . and he tried to influence everybody else to do the same.

As Mattie pulled the car in their driveway and put it in park, Conner unbuckled his seatbelt, jumped out of the car, and yelled for Biscuit. "Come here, buddy? Come here. Biscuit!" But Biscuit just wasn't biting. Instead he kept running down the street in the other direction, chasing another dog from the neighborhood. Conner grabbed his backpack and walked toward the front door, kicking the monkey grass as he waited on Mom to get her purse, a bag from Walgreens, and a brown box full of who-knows-what-else. As she walked up to the door with arms full, she and Conner could both now hear the home phone ringing from inside the kitchen and front guest bedroom—two rings, three rings, four rings . . .

In quick-search mode, Mattie dropped the box and bag as she scrambled on the stoop, trying to find the house keys she had just thrown into her purse for some crazy reason. She only had a million things in there, and she'd dumped half of them on the doormat by the time she located her keys in her bottomless bag. Her things scattering along the porch like marbles—just as she was losing her own—she pushed the door open. It banged against the doorstopper before ricocheting back, and she rushed to the phone already on its sixth or seventh ring. She was barely able to grab it before they hung up.

Conner, being the helper he was, walked into the kitchen carrying the brown box and Walgreens bag. Full of curiosity, he stopped at the kitchen table to see who was on the other end of the line. As he read his mother's facial expression and studied the look in her eyes, he knew something wasn't right. Mom's complexion was gathering a rapid dose of color.

"Mrs. Jones, this is Dr. Kozlowski's nurse, Anne Thomas, from Moses H. Cone Memorial in Greensboro, North Carolina. You have a son, Gaston Jones, correct?"

"Yes," a frantic Mattie responded.

"Last night or early this morning, he was in an accident off I-85 some forty-plus miles outside of Charlotte. We have him here in critical care on the fourth floor. He has some injuries and has been in and out of consciousness, even though he hasn't spoken to anyone at this time. We did decide to medically induce him into a coma to ensure the protection and control of the pressure dynamics of his brain. We hope to minimize the swelling and inflammation that way. We had a difficult time getting your contact information, but after we found Mr. Jones's identification at the crash site, Officer Brian Jennings, a state trooper, tried to call this number but didn't get an answer. He left a voicemail asking you to call his office. Did you receive that message?"

Mattie tried to control her breathing. "Unfortunately, no. We've had some problems with our answering machine over the last few days."

Struggling to make sense of it all, Mattie jotted down the contact information for the hospital with shaky fingers. As soon as the nurse hung up, Mattie called the airlines to book an immediate flight. Then she called Cassidy—her best friend and rock. In just a few rings, life had turned upside down—

again. She had faced adversity before, but nothing could compare to this sudden, devastating news about her oldest boy.

FOURTEEN

I am not what I ought to be, not what I want to be, not what I am going to be, but thankful that I am not what I used to be.
—John Wooden

Gaston's groggy mind had been moving in and out of consciousness for several hours, and during that time, he had heard only soft-spoken chatter between the doctors and nurses. What was going on? He couldn't piece any of it together. He had no idea where he was, why he was seeing what he saw...Nothing made sense, and furthermore, his brain couldn't stay awake long enough to figure it out. As he opened his eyes more fully than he had in weeks, he saw a person propped up in the corner of the room...wherever he was.

He tried so hard to gather bits and pieces from the dialogue he could hear. Did he hear them say there were unsure concerns if he would "make it" at one point? Had he been in a coma? As his eyelids stirred, he was still somewhat dazed and unable to talk. *How did I let this happen?* he thought to himself. *What is the last thing I remember?*

Gaston managed to open his eyes and take in more of the room around him. As he stirred, the first full words he heard clearly were something about "Beegee."

Gaston blinked and knew his brother must be in the room. The free-spirited Conner always seemed to put him in a comforting place—and boy did Gaston wish to be taken to a better one right now.

❖

Conner stood and examined the beeping machines and IVs, then turned square to face the bed. He slowly sat down next to Gaston's feet and rested his right arm over his left, gathering his thoughts and emotions. He began rubbing Gaston's left hand with his fingertips, gently back and forth, staring intently at his brother as if he were a rare diamond he had just found in the mines of South Africa. He wished Gaston could see what he saw. If only he'd known that Gaston wanted to be the man Conner believed he was...

Gaston's eyes were oh-so-slightly cracked open. The doctors had been weaning him off the drugs that had kept him in the induced coma, and his family had been there for the weeks since the wreck. Conner had no idea if his brother was awake or could see him, even though Mattie had told Conner that Gaston was in a deep sleep. Even so, nothing had stopped Conner from bringing his comforting message to his Beegee. He had purposeful words that he knew he had to share.

"Go ahead, honey, if you want to say something to him," said Mattie. "They're trying to wake him up, and I'm sure he's trying to listen. He might be able to take in what you want to say."

The uncomfortable silence was deafening. Gaston's heart pounded as he lay in the stillness of a moment that seemed frozen in time. Conner's big ol' smile thawed Gaston's coma with every minute, and as he blinked and focused he noticed his brother was sporting a maroon short-sleeved "Life Is Good" T-shirt. The screen-printed slogan told Gaston to "Do what you like. Like what you do." What a simple yet astonishing thought. Who had engineered such a profound slogan? It was as clear and direct a message as the one presented by the gentle-spirited lady from the car rental booth days before. How many days ago? Gaston had no way to know.

As Gaston's eyes opened wider, he took in the room filled wall to wall with invested doctors and nurses, no doubt all wondering what was about to take place. Gaston felt the anticipation on his skin and opened his mouth slightly—but even as he struggled to clear the fog from his brain, he could tell that everyone was looking at something else in the room. They were looking at his brother.

Conner cleared his throat and sat up straighter. Then he twisted his shoulders and glanced slowly around the room, commanding attention. He seemed to be making sure everyone was ready for what he had to say.

❖

"Shut the door, pwease!"
Someone tapped the door shut with a click.

Conner breathed a deep inhale, pausing before a long exhale . . . then again.

"Beegee, I hope yous can hear me . . . Can you? I knows your eyes are closed, but I must tell yous this anyways." He fixed his eyes on his brother's, now blinking.

"Beegee, does you remember Uncle Blandry? And does you remember that Reverend Shipley? I knows you do! Well, then you remembers that day after we got back from the funeral and you and I walked back to our room. Right?"

Gaston managed a slight nod.

"And does yous remember that we talked about how Reverend Shipley said some things that he thought were true about Uncle Blandry, and all the people that were there thought were true too? But we knew different. In Uncle Blandry's 'celebration of life moment,' the reverend pretended our uncle was a perfect example for all—a perfect father to his kids, a perfect husband to his wife . . . He pretended that Blandry was very involved in his church, was a devoted steward, and had his priorities in line. And that now he had gone to heaven." Conner closed his eyes and shook his head.

"Beegee, we knows better. That our uncle didn't live as good as he could've. He didn't go to church and didn't always do right. And that pastor was pretending that it's just a given or something—that we all goes to heaven when we die! Well, I am here to tell you, Beegee, that what he said wasn't true. What a joke! That was *not* a true message about Uncle Blandry. That was . . .

That was a clown's eulogy! That funeral misled people because it covered up, patched over who we knows our uncle was. Many of the people there knew it, and well... God does too.

"Uncle Blandry didn't know Jesus because he told us so. He thought there was a God but wasn't sure how it all worked. Beegee, we both know that there are too many people going through their lives not dealing with hurt, pain... They're faking it, misleading people, miserable, and so much more. Thinking they gots all this time, when one day... well, you know... They wants to get all things right before they get things rights with the Lord. But it don't work that way. Too many people are carrying so many burdens and regrets, sinking in sadness all while putting on a show.

"Folks hope they figure out their life before they lose their time. But while they're searching, their end of time may come! It always comes quicker than they wish. And if they aren't careful, they're goings to have someone standing up and doing the same thing they did for Uncle Blandry: giving them a clown's eulogy! It is a shame. It's a *tragedy*! Period! Why's people falling for this? A life of darkness that doesn't seek the light has no hope for the pearly gates—but maybe for them other gates. Everybody thinks all the deceased at a funeral are going to heaven. My Bible tells me that's not true."

Conner paused and looked around the room. He noticed his Aunt Cassidy, her head bowed, tears trickling down her face at the truth of what Conner had said about her late husband. He turned his attention back to his brother, whose eyes were fully open now. "Beegee. Understand me: You's my hero! You know I believe in living an authentic life. We need to be transparent and joyful when we succeed, and truthful when we trudge through the tough moments guaranteed in life. We's got to exemplify inner peace and be grateful with God's blessings, even during challenging times.

"I've been sitting around here waiting for you to get better, thinking about you and how much I been missing you. So even though now I knows you are gonna be okay, I decided to write your eulogy just in case you died. And of course it is not a clown's eulogy like Uncle Blandry's. I wrote it like a prayer, but not a finished one, because I knows you's not finished either. It makes me so proud. Simply, it goes like this:

"Dear Jesus, thank you for Beegee. Thank you for blessing me with a brother who is real and the best, happiest person I know. Thank you, Jesus, that he always loves me, cares for me, and lives his life as a great example of how life should be lived—with authenticity, with happiness and joy, and with peace and unconditional love. He has everything that any-one could ever want. One day, God, please let me grow up to be just like my brother. In your name I pray..."

❖

Before Conner pronounced his "amen," Gaston began choking with emotion to the point he could hardly breathe. His eyes were now open in more ways than one, and he wept in a way he hadn't wept since Cully died.

The skin on his body felt like tiny flames as he raised his arms, for the first time in many days, toward his brother. As the regret washed over him, Conner looked at him, stunned with amazement. Their eyes met as if they hadn't seen each other in thirty years, and Conner leaned over and embraced his brother with the strength of a lion. Not a dry eye in the room could've been found.

Gaston trembled as his mind searched for clarity and discernment. All he could gather was, *I'm not sure what all has happened, but if I have just one more chance from this moment forward, that's all I need.*

"Beegee, I thoughts we had lost you," a jubilant Conner blurted out.

"I needed you to find me," Gaston managed, his voice cracking. He felt as though his brother's words and embrace were rescuing him from his demons.

"Where have you been?" Conner continued. "Come on home. We been looking for you."

"Me too, Conner." Gaston took a deep breath. "I'm sure most have."

❖

Gaston, now fully awake and alert, was awestruck by the outpouring of love and support in the room. Mattie could barely contain her tears, overjoyed by her son's recovery—and she had given him a "welcome back" greeting of her own. But there was one individual left in the room whom he did not know. She had been perched off in the corner amid Conner's eye-opening speech, and after everyone else had slowly trickled out of the room, she approached Gaston's bed.

"Gaston, you must meet our new family friend, Anne Thomas," said Mattie. "She took good care of you after the accident and stayed in touch with us every day. She was your triage nurse and oversaw your critical care right after your wreck. She's an angel, and we—especially Conner—have been wanting you to meet her."

Stunned, Gaston could hardly concentrate on a response. His brain was still catching up, but even so, he was mesmerized by what he saw. After he failed to greet this angel, she said she had a long shift ahead of her and needed to go. She spoke briefly with Mattie and Aunt Cassidy, then gave them each a hug as well as a big one to Conner. Gaston didn't know the whole story about their past—about how she had tried to save his life—but he sure was hopeful for the future, even as she quietly walked out the door.

❖

Gaston's inner wheels turned a mile a minute. As he looked around his hospital room, and thought again about his brother's words, he knew this was the day his circus was officially over. Finally, with a committed heart, his life could begin. Miraculously, he had been given another chance to stop clowning before it was too late!

FIFTEEN

We ourselves feel that what we are doing is just a drop in the ocean. But if the drop was not in the ocean, I think the ocean would be less because of the missing drop.
—*Mother Teresa*

It was the hottest ticket in the history of the SHEADS Award. Just days after the announcement of the year's honored recipient, the event had sold out completely. The awards ceremony had even reached international acclaim with the help of the IDSC, the International Down Syndrome Coalition, among other partnering agencies—but the Jones family might've been the most excited attendants of all.

The evening of the event drew near, and Mattie, Conner, and Gaston donned their very best. Gaston—almost feeling like a new man by now—even sprang for a fancy black car, so the family could arrive at the fancy Washington DC hotel in style. As Gaston and Mattie took their seats at a table of honor, Gaston couldn't help but stare at his mother, whose smile stretched from ear to ear.

After the crowd mingled for a few minutes, shaking hands and slapping backs, a man in a tuxedo climbed the stage and adjusted the microphone. "Ladies and gentlemen, my name is Terry B. Byrne, and I am the committee chair for the National SHEADS Award. On behalf of the entire committee, I thank you for being here tonight. The National SHEADS Award is given annually to a recipient who has best exemplified the criteria in line with its founding father, Dr. William Sheads, and his lasting impact and contribution to society. Persons nominated in their respective communities must meet the criteria and be successful in their struggles while maintaining integrity and sense of purpose, while also honoring their differences when necessary. This year's recipient can be described as someone who can present his opinion while still honoring the voice of others. He is confident, honest with himself and others, and stands behind his beliefs while staying true to himself. He has never been one to conform to others' expectations of him. This person has found his distinctive voice and shows us all what it means to <u>live authentically</u>. His impact can be felt both near and far, and we can thank him for the betterment of society."

The gentleman paused and adjusted his black tie. "This evening, we are proud to have some special guests with us to bestow this award on a very special man. Before dinner is served, please join me in warmly welcoming those guests—President George W. Bush and First Lady Laura Bush!"

A door in the back of the ballroom opened, and in walked President Bush and the First Lady. Their security unit moved alongside them, and close behind came Dr. William Sheads and a beaming Conner

Jones. His eyes twinkled at the enthusiastic applause, and as he neared the front of the room he saw his very proud mother and his emotional brother. Conner had, and always would, make his big brother proud. Gaston had never been jealous of Conner, but he felt a touch of envy as he thought about all his brother had accomplished with his life. How would he ever have guessed that Conner would bring his family to such a place as this?

Upon reaching the stage, Dr. Sheads shook hands with the president and first lady before proudly draping an arm around his special friend's shoulders. Conner wore a shiny black tuxedo, a starched white shirt, and a royal blue bowtie and cummerbund. Bright lights and cameras were homed in on him as he and Dr. Sheads walked toward the sponsor table nearest the podium, all while sharing a genuine and private moment together.

Gaston and Conner both wished they could freeze the moment in time. Conner was the first-ever special needs recipient in the history of the award, and Gaston couldn't imagine anyone else being more deserving. As Conner took his seat at the dinner table with Dr. Sheads and President and Mrs. Bush, glasses were filled all around. He took a long, nervous sip from his goblet of tea, and his mouth watered as he read the menu in front of him: buttered lobster bites, edamame and herb salad, filet mignon, potato gratin, garlic and lemon charred broccoli, and a caramel pecan turtle cheesecake with vanilla bean ice cream. He tried to focus on his dinner company and the food placed before him, but he couldn't help but think about the speech he had prepared and practiced what felt like dozens of times.

The black-tie event attendees were served an amazing dinner, but nothing like what they were about to chew on in mere minutes. They would have plenty more to digest after hearing Conner's words!

SIXTEEN

*No one can do everything,
but everyone can do something.*
—*Max Lucado*

After the dessert had been served and Conner had relaxed somewhat, Mr. Byrne approached the podium yet again. "Wow, what a great meal tonight! Wasn't that just magnificent? I know all of you here will echo my sentiments in thanking those who have worked tirelessly to prepare such an amazing event for us to enjoy and remember." He paused as the crowd clapped in gratitude. "The committee thanks the SHEADS Award team members across the country who make sure all our regional, statewide, and of course our national award-winners know how special and valuable they are to their communities. We are grateful for the daily commitments they have made to impact the world we live in. Also, a sincere thanks to the local and national media outlets present who have promoted and reported upon this event tonight, which will be aired nationally on CBS and PBS. And lastly, we would be remiss if we didn't thank the wonderful team here at The Washington Hilton Hotel for hosting us.

"And yet, as good as that meal was, the best is yet to

come. We are in for a real treat! Without further ado, it is with tremendous honor and privilege—not only for me, but also for everyone affiliated with the SHEADS Award—to welcome such an admirable speaker and co-presenter tonight. Ladies and gentleman, please join me in giving a tremendously warm welcome to none other than the forty-third President of the United States of America, President George W. Bush!"

The audience applauded wildly as President Bush took the podium and shook Mr. Byrne's hand. Then he adjusted the mic and cleared his throat. "Thank you for your gracious acknowledgement and for asking Laura and me to be part of such an unparalleled event. For many years—as have many of you—I have followed this prestigious award and its winners, both on the local levels and all the way up to each year's national winner. I am amazed not only by the fortitude, desire, and character embodied by the nominees, but also their drive and dedication to be difference makers in our great nation and the larger world. It takes determination to reach such heights. It takes heart, selflessness, and perseverance. It takes vision and action, and an undeniable commitment to improving the world. Those nominated each year are trailblazers and heroes. They make our towns, cities, states, country, and our world a better place because of the choices they have made." President Bush paused a moment to turn his head toward a grinning Conner.

"Though many wonderful people were nominated this year," he continued, "only one can win. After spending some invaluable, unforgettable time together prior to dinner, and after hearing about the amazing contributions this particular individual has made, I am confident that he and his thriving organization are worthy of the award being bestowed upon him tonight. His platform is big, yet his heart is even bigger; and I know that what he wants to share with you tonight will forever change you, as well as Laura and me. Something about this night just feels a little extra special. And so, I would like to ask my good friend, the distinguished Dr. William Sheads, to please join me here at the podium to help introduce a deserving and admired man—the winner of the 2015 SHEADS Award."

Dr. Sheads stood tall as he shook the president's hand at the podium. President Bush leaned in for a few private words before motioning toward the microphone.

"First," began Dr. Sheads, "congratulations to all those nominated and to all the finalists. You are living examples of selflessness: human beings who care so much for others and want the best for them. Every year I am amazed by your contributions to society. Too many times your willingness to help others goes unpublicized or even unnoticed; but don't ever forget that your sacrifices have ripple effects that will eventually reach the river banks of strangers' lives. This year, it is my privilege and great honor to present Conner Dale Jones, who was unanimously chosen as the 2015 National SHEADS Award winner."

The standing-room-only crowd leapt to its feet, applauding so loudly that Conner could barely concentrate on walking to the podium. He heard "Hear,

hear!" and "Bravo, Conner!" from all sides of the room as he, in a daze, shook Dr. Sheads's hand, as well as the president's and the first lady's. It was now his turn to share a few chosen words.

Gaston screamed out with joy, tears overflowing with delight. His brother had made history! Conner Jones was not only the first-ever special needs recipient, but also the first-ever recipient with Down syndrome to even make the state finals since the award's inception in 1984. What a shining moment! Conner stood in front of a boisterous crowd of over twenty-seven hundred, not including the world media present and one very nervous fire marshal. Conner smiled broadly, and his rosy, chubby cheeks lifted his entire face. He stood patiently for about ninety seconds, quiet in disbelief and awe, soaking up the clapping and the whistling and hoping to lock it into his memory. Before beginning his speech, and before taking hold of his moment in the sun, he took a small sip of ice water and looked all around the room.

He waited respectfully as the crowd's applause tapered down and the few who had left their seats hurriedly returned from wherever they had strayed. Their eyes were focused on the man who maybe didn't look like them or talk like them, but who, for all intents and purposes, was just like them. Nothing seemed to be plainer in Conner's mind than the message he was about to deliver tonight. The room went silent as Conner further adjusted the downwardly tilted microphone, preparing for what they weren't prepared for. Conner's life would never be the same, and neither would theirs after the magical speech he had prepared for this magical night.

❖

"I learned from *The Velveteen Rabbit* that yous can't be ugly if yous are real—except to people to who don't understand. Years ago, I decided I was a son and brother seeking to be his own person . . . just hoping for a chance to try! I did not start out hoping to be in the limelight; I only wanted to share the light I had. This moment, this night, is bigger than me. As yous can sees, I am a little fella, or not as big as most—but I do have opportunities, just as yous do, to shine my light onto others. Then hopefully, that light will help them to see where theys can go. I do that through love.

"I never wanted to be laughed at for how I looked or made fun of for what I was born with. I's been ridiculed, isolated, rejected, and left out of some fun things because of . . . well, because some people have decided that I am a funny-looking person that they can't relate to. Mainly, people choose not to give me the benefit of the doubt. Me? I hears them all: *Big head, short fat boy, you're not one of us* . . . Yous probably heard the hecklers too.

"Through all the noise, I heard one day that I was uniquely and intentionally made by God. Folks' mean words were just self-fulfilling chatter. I also understood that their words could not be harmful unless given permission . . . by me and by you. I decided not to buy in because I know we *all* matter. We *all* are important, and we *all* have special talents to share. Every person here can make an impact in the lives of others. That's what I know. That's what I choose!"

❖

The crowd sat enraptured. Gaston choked back tears and leaned forward in his seat, taking in every single word that worked its way out of Conner's smiling face. No one is perfect, but Gaston sure looked at his brother as he would've an angel. As his eyes swept around the room, he took in the other rapt faces in the audience ... But he never could've expected in a million years to see what his eyes landed on in the very back of the room.

SEVENTEEN

There is very little difference in people.
But that little difference makes a big difference.
—W. Clement Stone

Nothing had been predictable about this night. Just as Conner was positioning himself to give his knock-out moving remarks, a tall, slender, and very attractive blonde slipped quietly through a set of double doors. Very eloquently dressed, she had stepped in to get a glimpse of the president and to hear what Conner had to say—but unintentionally, she became the full focus of Gaston's attention when his eyes sensed movement along the side of the room. She moved quietly along the far wall, wearing a full-length rose-colored dress with sparkling sequins. The golden light from the chandelier shimmered against her stilettos. Only she shined brighter than Gaston's face as recogni-tion dawned on him—that he had seen this stunning blonde before, who now stood off to the side of the room near the twelve-foot Brazilian mahogany pillars that decorated the walls of the ballroom.

An exhilarating sensation flew through Gaston's body. A double take—and maybe a triple—was needed to actually confirm what he was seeing. *No way ... Could this be true? Is this really happening?* He knew that smile! It had already been a dream night, but really . . . His mind raced, and almost as soon as his thoughts caught up with him the woman's gaze locked with his. She raised a gentle hand and waved slowly back and forth at him, grinning from ear to ear. She craned her neck, trying to take in the vibrant mass of people now standing, their thunderous applause erupting for the man of the hour. Gaston could hardly take it all in himself. What was Anne Thomas doing there?

❖

Conner, too, had noticed the pretty nurse making her way through the room—but he still had a few words to say. So he took another sip of water and carried on.

"I's so excited," he said, "because so many imperfect human beings have shown up tonight. For the record, yous ladies and gentlemen sure are keeping me up late, past my bedtime." The crowd chuckled at Conner's joke, and he smiled, pleased.

"With a truthful and heavy heart, I must admit it's a shame, though, because most of you here are probably feeling stuck! Maybe yous had hoped for a perfect world and to be perfect in it, and due to your shortcomings, things didn't turn out as planned. In other words, life happened! And now, far too many of you are still waiting . . . and waiting . . . just hoping for your real life to begin. But the truth is, we don't get mulligans. The life you're living today is the only one you have!

"Seeking the forgiveness that you hasn't even granted yourself or given others, your days now consist of piling on more and more for your future plans. You expect a happy fairy-tale ending, but you have less time than ever before. Your never-ending to-do list and your calendars full of plans make much of the future, but nothing of today. Your unfulfilled dreams stay that way, mainly because yous can't seem to get past your failures, your shortcomings, or your disappointments.

"Yeah, maybe yous got your promotions and bonuses, but your plate is so full of self yous got no time for others unless they're going your way. You say, 'In due time, I will!' But for now all yous want is a little bit more . . . more money, awards, and achievements. You want to be able to say, 'I finally made it!' The honest truth? Yous will never make it until to you stop focusing on yourself and start focusing on others. People out there are desperate for the greatest things you can give them: your love and your time. You may think yous have time to start giving of yourself tomorrow, but didn't you say that yesterday, and the day before that? And the day before that?

"Our best intentions need attention! Don't miss the moments, the chances to say 'I love yous' to the people who needs to hear it. Don't miss every opportunity to serve the less fortunate and neglected, like the orphans, the widows, and the poor.

"A wise man once shared with me his thoughts on the Day of Judgment after we die. He believed that for some folks, when they arrive in heaven, they'll see miles of boxes there, warehouses full of missed blessings. Then God will point to the boxes and say, 'These fortunes and opportunities could've been yours on earth, if only yous had done what I had created yous to do. But you chose otherwise: to be who the world told yous to be.'

"Your story is part of God's bigger story—but God needs each of us to do our part. I have read the statistics and know that most of you are supposed to be here on earth more years than me. But will yous truly *live* more years or just blow out a few more candles? You have the chance to fly, and to take others with yous to new heights. To see and experience things you never knew existed. Don't miss out on the things yous *could* have done. Even more, don't miss out on what you could've given to others. Don't neglect the gifts yous got to give!

"Yous are the only person with your unique abilities. I am reminded of the shiny paint cans that sit on shelves all around the world. Inside are beautiful colors and finishes, but if the cans are never opened, over time theys will dry up and become useless. What is the special paint color inside your can? God has given us the brushes we need to paint a masterpiece, but it is up to us to do it. Your one-in-a-million painting can brings strength, hope, and encouragement to others. Far too many are blessed with so much and have done so little with it. Maybe some of yous are sitting here thinking, *Conner, I've got nothing.* And yous would be right. You have *nothing* to *lose*! Don't waste another minute. For too many, time gobbles them up before their 'one day' ever happens.

"So—are you stuck? Be true to yourself and to others. With discipline and determination, keep going.

Get up, respond to the call. Journey to the freedom yous deserve, and finish well!"

Conner paused and gazed one last time around the room, preparing himself to deliver his last remarks. He inhaled and looked back down at his notes.

"If you believe one thing tonight, if you hears one thing tonight, hears this: Your future is now. So, what will your next step be? All we have is time, but the question is, *How much?* I believe that if yous start right now, you have time to make a difference. Remember what I learned from *The Velveteen Rabbit* that yous can't be ugly if yous are real? We all know we's not ugly, so let's make sure we are real. I love and believe in yous! May God bless yous, your family, and your future as yous go on living intentionally, living authentically, and blessing others as much as you can. Make it fun or funny. Make a difference. It's a choice!"

The crowd roared and leapt to their feet as Conner stepped away from the podium, having reminded the audience of Dr. Sheads's token phrase. As Conner looked for where to go next, he was greeted by slaps on the back and handshakes from Terry B. Byrne, Dr. Sheads, and even the president himself. Mrs. Bush stood from her seat of honor and congratulated him too, whispering in his ear how much she had enjoyed his speech. And as Conner basked in the glow of the night, he looked down and caught the eyes of his family—his sweet mother, Mattie Jones, and his best friend and big brother, his Beegee. They both stood and clapped with all their might.

❖

Gaston was overwhelmed by the noise and the joy of his brother's big moment. Not to mention, he couldn't quite understand why Anne—the nurse who had saved him—had made such a stunning appearance. As he glanced toward the front of the room where she had stood, he noticed her moving toward the back of the room, as if planning to leave before the crowd.

Gaston panicked. Before he knew it, he was hurriedly weaving in and out of couples, trying to intercept her as she made her way to the exit. Anxiety flooded his body as he attempted to keep her in his line of sight amid the mass of partygoers. His heartbeat sped up as he wondered if she would really care what he had to say. In fact, what *was* he going to say?

Before Anne reached the back doors, a security man approached her. From a distance, Gaston saw a look of confusion and possibly fear on her face. Gaston broke out into a near-sprint.

As he got close enough, he heard the black-suited, earpiece-wearing, barrel-chested man asking her if she had a ticket for the event. Had she sneaked past security? Had she inadvertently broken protocol? Before Anne could explain, Gaston reached them and waved the all-access VIP pass draped around his neck. "She's okay. She's with me," he said breathlessly.

The Secret Service agent seemed satisfied with that. "Okay, sir. Security's very tight whenever Mr.

President's involved." He gave a quick nod and moved back toward the room's exit doors.

Gaston stared at Anne, speechless—though this was not the first time she had seen him that way. Without a word, he reached around her and squeezed her tight, and she returned the embrace. He just couldn't turn her loose, nor did he want to. When they finally did pull apart, their eyes locked. He had presumed he would never see her again after his hospital stay had ended. Little did he know how many prayers and kind words of encouragement she had poured over him while he was asleep.

Mattie, staring from a distance, gleamed with joy and shock as she witnessed the embrace of her oldest and the friend who had helped them in their greatest time of need.

❖

Gaston had to take a few deep breaths to compose himself. "What are you doing here?" he asked Anne. "I just never . . . But here you are. I can't believe you came all this way . . . I assumed I'd never hear your voice or see your gorgeous ocean-blue eyes ever again. How did this just happen? This has to be a dream. I've wanted to call you for months but had no clue how to get hold of you."

"Well, your mother invited me tonight," said Anne. "She could've given you my number." She winked, and Gaston's insides melted.

"Well, maybe my brain is still healing because that

didn't once occur to me." He closed his eyes in embarrassment. "But no matter. You're here now—the caregiver who went above and beyond and made sure I stayed alive."

He paused again, struggling toward the next words. "Anne, will you ... will you ... will you let me take you out sometime? If nothing else, I owe it to you."

Surprised filled her eyes. "Well, I had hoped you might ask me something like that, but honestly I never thought we would ever have an opportunity like this. You're a walking miracle, Gaston ... and I'm glad."

The gleeful and breathtaking blonde took Gaston's hand and squeezed it. He was so nearly paralyzed by her response, by everything that was transpiring, that he shielded his eyes with his free hand. Then she leaned forward and connected her arms around his neck, her nose brushing against his as they embraced once more. Gaston was so astonished by the moment that he felt himself looking from the outside in, as if he were a photographer zooming in on the two of them for the climax of a Hollywood film.

Gaston's giddy smile matched hers, and they both enjoyed a laugh, as if asking each other, "Is this really happening?" Still in disbelief, he smoothly leaned over and kissed her on the left cheek. Taking a step back, his locked eyes with hers and fought back the tears that had threatened through the long, emotional night.

"I want to get to know *you*, Gaston," she said.

"Me too. You don't know how much this means to me!"

❖

Gaston and Anne's reunion felt frozen in time, but to those observing, it had been merely a brief encounter. For the minutes that felt to them like an hour, the crowd had continued their thunderous standing ovation. Conner's speech had given people more than their surf-and-turf to digest. The attendees were moved to tears by the heartfelt and honest message from Conner "Little Something Extra" Jones's words truly had delivered. No one in attendance would forget this night—especially Conner Dale Jones. He had started something big years before, and now he expected others to finish. As he saw it, everyone had a part to play in the world.

❖

Gaston saw a jubilant Conner out of the corner of his eye. He didn't want to leave Anne's side, but he didn't want to miss meeting President Bush either. So he reached into his coat pocket and pulled out a card, then handed it to Anne.

"Here is my cell number. I won't be working with this company much longer, thank goodness, but the cell phone still works. I'm going make some changes, figure out a way to stay closer to home." He paused and gazed into her eyes once more. "I really hate to say goodbye for now, but I've got to get to the stage to meet the president and take a photo with Conner and Dr.

Sheads. Or even better, can you possibly stick around here for just a few more minutes? I hope you'll stay or at least call. Please?"

She smiled as she placed the card in her clutch and closed it with a click. "I promise to call."

Gaston gave her shoulder a gentle squeeze, then he began weaving his way back through the lingering crowd. Mattie gave him a sly wink as he came closer to the stage where she and Conner waited patiently. The Secret Service watched intently as Gaston walked up the remaining steps and across the stage to approach Conner and Mattie, Dr. Sheads, President Bush, and Laura Bush. The special honoree could not have been prouder to introduce his Beegee to his heroes, saying, "This is my big brother Gaston, and I'm so prouds of him. He's the best big brother there is. He's the reason I am here today."

Gaston was humbled by his brother's introduction, but he shook hands with them all before taking his place next to Conner for a photograph. He could hardly believe that this was their life, their moment as a family. He wished for a passing moment that Cully could've been there to say some proud words over his youngest boy, but then he said a silent prayer of thanks.

Conner reached up and draped his arm proudly over his brother's shoulder before he turned to the camera and smiled. The Jones family beamed as the camera clicked and clicked, locking the moment into a photograph. Before President Bush was escorted off stage, he approached Conner one more time.

"Conner, again, amazing job tonight. Your profound message was moving to us all. It was truly an honor to be here to celebrate with you and your family. Thank you for what you've done for your community and this entire nation. It takes courage to do all you've done. It takes courage to do something great!"

Without hesitation, Conner took the president's hand. "Thank you, sir. Courage is what me must have and give away. By choosing to encourage people, we have chosen to give them the greatest gift: *hope!* My prayer is that yous and Mrs. Bush will keep hope alive. Thank yous for making this special moment . . . well, special, sir. I know yous didn't have to be here, and I will be forever gratefuls."

Mrs. Bush gave him one last quick hug before she and the President were escorted out. Conner knew it was a defining moment, but to him, weren't they all?

EIGHTEEN

*It was one of the best days of my life,
a day during which
I lived my life and didn't think about my life at all.*
—Jonathan Safran Foer

The line of attendees wrapped around the ballroom, waiting for the chance to congratulate, shake hands with, or hug Conner Jones. Many waited patiently to tell him of the impact he'd made on them tonight. After nearly an hour, the room finally began to thin.

"Conner Dale Jones," said an emotional Gaston, bear-hugging the new SHEADS Award winner. He held onto his brother for some time before slowly releasing him. "You are so awesome, and I am so proud of you. You're my hero! Thank you, Conner, for saving my life . . . and after tonight's words, I bet you've saved a few more. I know what the road to dying looks and feels like. Thanks for introducing me to a new one."

Gaston cleared his throat and took his brother by the shoulders. "If it's okay with you, I'm excited to start down the road of living. I want to work with an amazing team and the awesome creator of 47 Matters . . . if you will let me."

"Of course!" said the jubilant, smiling Conner.

"And, oh, by the way . . . just you and me are going back next month to the special place Daddy always wanted to take us," said Gaston. "It's all on me, and we are going to have a blast."

❖

The sun glittered across a piece of the more than forty-three thousand acres of boaters and fishermen's paradise, as small rippling waves tapped against a sixteen-foot aluminum johnboat. For the first time in a very long time, Gaston could visualize a spectacular reflection off the near-perfect smooth surface. Thirty-one days and one hundred and nineteen miles later, everything seemed to be trending back upright for Gaston—with the exception of the red-and-white bobber sinking out of sight as Conner landed another "slab." The serene, picturesque day on Pickwick Lake had been a tremendously successful one, as the once full bucket of crappie minnows neared empty. Roughly fifty crappie, a couple of large mouths, and a few chinquapins now filled the YETI Tundra 210 cooler.

In celebration of Conner's award, the two brothers had picked one of The Landings' new, relaxing cabins, which rested seventy-five feet off in the pines and overlooked tranquility—a quality Gaston had overlooked most of his life. After a satisfying day on the water, the deep fryer was popping as they cooked cornmeal and buttermilk dipped fish, along with some sweet and spicy hush puppies. As the sun set off to the west just beyond the Brian Brown Marina and a blended row of hardwoods and tall pines, Conner observed a grey heron gliding two feet over the water, looking for something appealing to eat before—

Well, before Gaston popped open a bottle of Barefoot Riesling. He wanted to talk about some thoughts he had been drowning in for some time. Moved with emotion and wondering how he should pour out this heaviness, his lips began to quiver. The wood creaked as Conner's rocker went back and forth across the wooden planks. He was focused on his hero, his Beegee, who joined him, glass in hand, on the next rocker over. The air was thick with anticipation until a *buuuuurp* from Conner slipped out and earned some giggles.

"Conner, it's been awhile since we wetted a hook. Been way too long, matter of fact, for a lot of things," Gaston said as he took a sip and a look around. "We got some catching up to do. And believe it or not, I'm finally going to stop running. Your old Beegee hasn't been at his best. I haven't been a good big brother. Bottom line is, I'm not really sure who I had let myself become ... but I am very sorry. Will you please forgive me?"

Conner was startled by the question. He stared at the ground, trying to process.

"Wake-up calls come at different times in life," Gaston continued, "if you are so lucky as to get one. Quite frankly, I was one of the lucky ones—and you played a big part in that, Conner. I know the Good Lord still has me here for a reason, so I guess He is not finished with me yet. Basically, you saved me—and I am forever grateful."

"Saved? Not sure how I did that, Beegee. All's I'z was being was myself. That's a God thing," replied Conner, gently lifting his head.

"Conner, I owe you more than you will ever know. Your actions have always spoken so loud on how life should be lived. And then, of course, your SHEADS Award speech validated it. And just so you know, I'm not the real hero. It's you, Conner Dale Jones."

As the beaming Conner stared at his big brother, Gaston unzipped his forest green and charcoal Columbia fleece and threw it to open and off with a flourish. Underneath was a short-sleeved undershirt that read in bold print: "Life is Good. Do what you like. Like what you do." As Gaston slowly turned around, his brother saw that the back read: "Conner Matters!"

Make it fun or funny.

Make a difference.

It's a choice!

A NOTE FROM THE AUTHOR

We all have a story,
so tell yours!

As the years seem to roll by fast, like the credits at the end of a movie, I have realized one thing is for sure; history repeats itself if we allow it to. Over the years, I've experienced far too many trading freedom and future for past and paralysis.

Have you found yourself letting the world name you, telling you who and what you need to become? You can't let culture define you. It's hard to fight an enemy who has a permitted fort in your head. Whether you have tried to copy someone else's life, or just live in bondage of previous failures; the past is history. Shallow friendships and numbness are symptoms of hiding secretive ways—but you do not have to tell yourself lies any longer. For too long, far too many have become disconnected from their environment, their relationships, and more importantly, from themselves. If this is you, you now must ask yourself: do I continue to let the past define me, or do I choose to forgive self and be released from my previous shackled old ways? You don't have to keep taping the broken pieces of your heart together. I know you didn't intend for your life to get screwed up, but you can straighten it up.

There is so much hope and great opportunity right in front of you. You can begin looking at life from a different perspective—one of reflection and new growth. The person you see in the mirror can decide to make the change for a happy and joyful rest of the story by painting a new and beautiful canvas with your very own and talented masterpiece brush. The lighted path out of darkness begins now. Why? Because you matter and people want to light their candle to your newfound way and the testimony from your previous experiences that will be so influential and impactful.

Let's be honest. Is it easy? NO. Long overdue? YES! And yes, it requires you to take a seemingly terrified first small step and committing to living authentically. One with boundless energy fueled with purpose, passion, and endless blessings. Hope is not lost, yet just beginning. You're 100 percent worth it, because you matter. Freedom starts now by lifting the lid blinding your eyes and heart, and letting God in to reveal a beautiful and amazing you that you were created for.

There is an old saying: "If we lived better, we wouldn't have to talk about it as much." We have to reframe our expectations, realign our priorities, rethink what is possible, and reconsider our ambitions. Have the certainty to press forward forging a new path. You are unique for a reason. Believe it! Your uniqueness is a great thing! You must finish the race and complete the task at hand. You are the only person in the whole wide world who can live your life and create new life-fulfilling and life-changing experiences.

When I was young, one of my best and most exciting discoveries was realizing that hide-and-seek is a fun game. And over time, I learned that being found is the best part of the game. In the game of life, people are searching, seeking you out. Unfortunately, many of you have not been found yet. That can feel very frustrating; but in order to be found, you have to find yourself first.

Great news! You're reading this, so the game is not over! Starting today, forgive yourself and change the world—one person, one moment at a time, beginning right now! Change leads to clues . . . and clues lead to success. You have meaning and are equipped for greatness. Believe in yourself and expect great things from yourself moving forward. Your time is now, so seize every day with all of your energy. Live a purposeful life—the one you were created for (the life only you can live)!

I know you can, and I know you will . . . because I believe in you!

> Sincerely,
> Kirk Tinsley

"For I know the plans I have for you," declares the LORD, *"plans to prosper you and not to harm you, plans to give you hope and a future."*
—*Jeremiah 29:11*

ACKNOWLEDGMENTS

First, this book is dedicated to my amazing wife, Lina, and our three boys: Kael, Elyas, and Levi for their unwavering support and love; to our wonderful Barbara (Paul) Smith for being a champion for this book to be written; for my mom, Sue, and her encouragement throughout the process; for my dad, Dale, and his important impact (even in his brief thirty-one years of life). I know he would be proud of his son for giving others hope. To Dick and Kathy Rollins for stepping in the gap and having an important part in my life; my brother, Terry Tinsley and family; Jorge and Martha Londoño, and Ale Londoño and family for their unconditional support; special friend and photographer Amy Conner Photography, for the prayer warrior family; the Byrnes; and last but not least, God, for not giving up on one of his wandering sheep and getting me through so much in my life to be able to give back, give hope, and impact His Kingdom!

Also, I would like to thank Robert D. Smith for his wise counsel and wisdom; my very talented editor, Jocelyn Bailey; contributors David Bennett, Renee Chavez, and Anne Severance; and creative cover designer, John Robinson.

Finally, this book was in the incubator for numerous years, therefore, so many have been impactful and I am forever grateful. Some will find their names sprinkled throughout the storyline characters in a token of my gratitude.

ABOUT THE AUTHOR

Kirk Tinsley is a powerful and inspiring speaker, author, and professional life coach who is widely recognized for his candid and inspiring talks that challenge and aid change through principles, perspective, and charted results. He gets the privilege of purposefully and passionately helping develop positive leaders while working alongside businesses, sports teams, professional athletes and entertainers, non-profits, and faith-based organizations. One of Kirk's main purposes is to transparently and authentically impact others by challenging, inspiring, and helping raise them up for a great and remarkable life—here and after for the Kingdom. That is why Kirk dedicates so much of his time to giving back, giving hope, and delivering hard truths and perspective when he is not enjoying time and laughter with his beautiful wife and three amazing boys.

Made in the USA
Columbia, SC
21 November 2020